"But I know, too, that God has blessed us and many others with this cave," she went on.

"I don't believe the cave is a curse. I believe it's a blessing."

"It can't be both. To you a blessing; to me a curse. We can't both be right, and we can't both be wrong."

They sat in silence together, listening to the water play a melody over the rocks. "Then we must come to a truce," Susanna declared, offering him her hand.

"A truce?" He took her hand in his.

"That while we may disagree, we can still respect and understand each other with God's help."

And maybe even more, he thought silently. He gazed at her hand, tiny, velvety white against his rough skin. He never felt anything so soft. He held onto it, savoring it. His thumb gently began caressing the top of her hand.

Her cheeks pinked. Her hand shifted in his. "Jared?" she asked softly.

The feel of her hand. The look of her face. Eyes blue like the feathers of a bluebird. Parted lips so inviting. Dare he even think of kissing her? Dare he consider her in such a fashion, one he could come to know, love, and even marry? He dropped her hand and stared off into the distance.

LAURALEE BLISS, a former nurse, is a prolific writer of inspirational fiction, as well as a home educator. She resides with her family near Charlottesville, Virginia, in the foothills of the Blue Ridge Mountains—a place of inspiration for many of her contemporary and historical novels. Lauralee Bliss writes inspirational fiction to provide readers with entertaining stories, intertwined with Christian principles to assist them in their day-to-day walk with the Lord. Aside from writing, she enjoys gardening, cross-stitching, reading, roaming yard sales, and traveling. Lauralee invites you to visit her Web site at www.lauraleebliss.com.

Books by Lauralee Bliss

HEARTSONG PRESENTS
HP249—Mountaintop
HP333—Behind the Mask
HP457—A Rose Among Thorns
HP538—A Storybook Finish
HP569—Ageless Love
HP622—Time Will Tell
HP681—The Wish

Into the Deep

Lauralee Bliss

Heartsong Presents

To Tracie who believed in my historical writing. Thank you for your support.

My heartfelt thanks to park rangers Vickie Carson and Joy Lyons of Mammoth Cave National Park for all their help and insight.

Special thanks to my husband, Steve, who tirelessly spent days making phone calls and arranging for a special cave tour and information.

A note from the Author:
I love to hear from my readers! You may correspond with me by writing:

Lauralee Bliss
Author Relations
PO Box 721
Uhrichsville, OH 44683

ISBN 1-59789-001-4

INTO THE DEEP

All scripture quotations are taken from the King James Version of the Bible.

Our mission is to publish and distribute inspirational products offering exceptional value and biblical encouragement to the masses.

PRINTED IN THE U.S.A.

one

Kentucky, 1843

A bang on the door awoke Jared Edwards in a start. He rubbed the sleep from his eyes and gazed out the window to see the faint rays of a new dawn just beginning to brighten the sky. He struggled to stand, even as a yawn broke across his face. Shuffling to the fireplace, he lit a candle from a banked ember. It was time he got up anyway. The cow needed milking, and he promised Uncle Dwight he would help plow up the fields.

Jared came to the door, still bleary-eyed from sleep, to find the shadowy image of his uncle standing outside. The man's nightshirt hung out of his pants, which he had obviously donned in haste. The silhouette of horses hitched to a wagon stood against the backdrop of the rising sun. Within the wagon were piles of quilts and what appeared to be his Aunt Mattie's trunk.

"Something's wrong, Jared."

Instantly, he found himself alert. "What? What's the matter, Uncle?"

The older man was visibly trembling. Jared stepped aside to allow him in. "It's Mattie. Someone came by to tell me she's doing very poorly. She's in a deep sleep and won't wake up."

Jared stared. *How can that be?* They had only left Mattie a short time ago in Dr. Croghan's care.

"We're going to the cave just as soon as you're ready." Uncle

Dwight shuffled inside. He sat down heavily at the small table that Jared had pieced together with leftover oak planks. He ran fingers through his brown hair streaked with gray. "Why did I let you talk me into taking her to that terrible place? A cave of all things! Mattie was safe here. She was happy. She had me to take care of her and not some strange doctor." He again ran his fingers through his hair. "I have to get her out of there. She needs to leave that place and come home."

Jared bit his lip as he headed to the back room to put on some clothes. Just yesterday, when he visited his uncle's place, he found Uncle Dwight staring at a small portrait of Aunt Mattie as a young woman. His stubby finger traced every part of her features while his blue eyes filled with tears. Even then Jared began questioning the decision he had made. But in his opinion, they had no choice. If they didn't do something, Mattie would have surely died.

When Jared heard that Dr. Croghan had built huts inside a nearby cave to help cure those sick with consumption, he had immediately gone to inquire. Standing there among the curious onlookers, he saw the man with his head held high, his strong voice echoing in the wooded glade.

"Mammoth Cave has given proof of its magical qualities," Dr. Croghan had stated to the awestruck throng massed before him. "As you know, we have found the human remains of Indians perfectly preserved within the cave, without a hint of decay. We have found the air to be of a constant temperature and humidity. And in Mammoth Cave, I have built cottages where the invalids may be cured of their pulmonary affections, rheumatism, even diseases of the eye. And I say that it will do far better for them than any medicine an apothecary can dispense."

Raucous applause accompanied the cheers. What the good

doctor described was nothing short of a miracle from on high. Jared couldn't wait to tell Uncle Dwight what he had learned.

When he came home that night, he found his dear aunt doubled over in a coughing spell, clutching a lacy handkerchief tinged with bright red blood—the telltale sign of the dreadful disease that had plagued her for several months. He immediately told his uncle the doctor's claims that the cave could cure Aunt Mattie's consumption. "This must be the answer we've been praying for."

"By putting her in some dark cave?" Dwight frowned, shaking his head, his broad forehead creased in worry.

"How else could Indians from long ago be kept without decay as the doctor said? The air in the cave must have something miraculous in it. We have to try, Uncle. If we don't do something, she'll die."

"But Mattie will be so far away from me. So far away." He looked back at the bedroom door slightly ajar. The sounds of her hacking cough echoed from within. "Can I visit her there?"

Jared shook his head. "Not from what I hear, not while she's in the cave anyway. It won't be long until she starts feeling better. Then she'll be home."

"Mattie and I haven't been separated since the day we were married. We've always been together, through the good and the bad. Even when the good Lord didn't give us children, at least we had each other."

Jared sighed. "But the only way you can stay together is if she gets well," he continued in earnest. "Please, Uncle. I believe this is the answer."

A look of resignation finally fell over his uncle's weary features. "All right, I will let her go for a short time. Better we are parted now than forever. And you've always had a good head about things, Jared. Better than that brother of mine who takes his family off to some strange place. I'm mighty glad you didn't go with them. I don't know what we would do without you."

❧

Jared hoped that same trust his uncle had laid in him back then, when he agreed to take his Aunt Mattie to the cave, still remained today, with this latest news of his aunt's deteriorating health. He feared a worse fate might have befallen them, a fate more dreadful than the consumption itself. He yanked on a pair of broadcloth trousers and shrugged into a shirt and coat. He stomped his feet into a pair of leather boots and lit a lantern with his shaky hand. *What if Aunt Mattie dies?* The mere thought made him shudder. *God, please help her. She can't die. She can't.*

He ventured into the main cabin where his uncle still sat, staring into the fire. "I'm bringing her back here," Dwight barked. "No use talking me out of it. Mattie's coming home with me. No more doctors and no more living in that cave."

Jared said nothing. The sun had barely begun to reveal the tip of its golden head when they stepped outside. A faint mist hung over the rolling Kentucky landscape. A distinct pattern of lantern light glowed in the distance as neighboring families went about their morning chores. Jared and his uncle climbed onto the jockey seat of the wagon. Jared took the reins and ushered the horses to the main road that led toward the cave.

"I don't care what you say," Uncle Dwight continued. "I know you told me to do this. But if she's getting worse, what are we gonna do?"

Jared had no answer. Without a miracle, Mattie would die—whether in the cave or at home. But he prayed it was not the former. Many times Jared sought the Lord for a miracle that would revive his aunt. Dr. Croghan and his cave seemed God's perfect answer.

The creaking of the wagon along the rutted road provided a sad serenade to the ride, its melancholy tune broken only by an occasional bird singing merrily from an overhanging tree limb. Jared wished for the right words to say to comfort his uncle, but his mind was a blank. Maybe he should tell his uncle to keep praying and trusting in the Lord.

Long ago, Jared explained to his uncle how, after a preacher on horseback shared with him the message of the Savior's love, Jared accepted Christ as his personal Savior. It was the power of Jared's rebirth, experienced here in Kentucky, which kept him home while his father took his siblings and mother and headed for St. Louis. His father had grown weary of trying to make a living in the exhausted Kentucky soil. Uncle Dwight thought his brother foolish to leave, and he told him so. Dwight then begged Jared to stay on and help him keep up the farm. At first, Jared found the prospect of leaving this place for another intriguing. But he also loved Ol' Kentuck. Not only had he been born here physically but spiritually, as well. This land had left its imprint on his heart and soul. And here he stayed to help his aunt and uncle and to live out his own life, by the grace of God.

It was midmorning by the time they reached the Mammoth Hotel, where visitors came to rest, eat a good meal, and take tours of the famous cave nearby. He had not yet stopped the wagon when an attractive woman bounded from the hotel entrance, her face all smiles. She wore a large straw hat tied with a blue ribbon. The white lawn of her dress, peeking out from beneath the dark cloak, shimmered like new-fallen snow in early winter. She was a vision of bright sunshine on a cool, foggy morning.

"Good morning. And how are you this fine day?"

Jared stared, taken aback by the cheery greeting on a somber day like today.

"We are about ready to leave for the first tour of Mammoth Cave this morning," she went on. "Only fifty cents for the short tour. And it is the most popular."

Fifty cents! Who has that kind of money to spend on a hole in the ground? "We aren't here for any tour," Jared stated flatly. "We came to see Dr. Croghan."

She stepped back as if surprised they were not going to be a part of some frolic within the cavern depths. "I'm sorry. The doctor is inside the cave at the moment, caring for the poor invalids."

"One of them is my aunt. We were told she is very ill. Please send for him."

She stood there as if uncertain what she should do. Finally, she whirled, her cloak billowing about her like a dark cloud. A trace of the sweet scent she wore lingered in the air and reminded him of wildflowers amid the tall grass. Jared had to admit that women were not in the forefront of his thoughts these days. He had too much work to do, what with tending to his place and looking after Uncle Dwight's fields. But the brief encounter with this lovely lady—her smiles, her charm, her beauty—awakened something within him, something he would have liked to consider further were it not for his concerns over Aunt Mattie and the farms to tend.

Jared turned his sights back to the hotel into which she had disappeared. Built close to the famous hole in the ground, the hotel formed an impressive sight, comprised of many wooden dwellings, some with several floors. No doubt the young woman knew little of a farmer's life. She had grown up wearing fancy frocks and spending her days in large rooms with fine furniture. He lived in his own small two-room cabin that he and his uncle built by the sweat of their brow. The furniture was handmade. The only items of finery were those provided by Aunt Mattie to "spruce up the place and make it more of a home," as she would say. Lace doilies, a tablecloth she had sewn, a quilt on the straw-filled bed, and occasionally, a vase filled with flowers gathered from the meadow. He couldn't imagine the fine lady he'd just seen living in his humble cabin, even walking with him down some path or sharing in a wagon ride under the rays of the fading sun. They were far too different, like night was to day.

Jared sat still in the wagon seat, fiddling with the leather reins. Beside him, Uncle Dwight had not uttered a word. While they waited, Jared saw the wide road leading down to the cave's entrance. It beckoned him and the other visitors to come and enter the murky depths. What was it about this cave that tempted people to pay good money to behold? He had to admit there was a strange lure to it. It drew him in a way he did not understand. Maybe it was the excitement of the unknown, of a new place he had never laid eyes on and existing right beneath his feet.

But at that moment, the lure of a hole in the ground paled in comparison to his concern for Aunt Mattie's failing health. A hard lump filled his throat. What would he do if something happened to her? What would his uncle say?

"Uncle, I'm going to see if I can find this Dr. Croghan myself." Jared jumped to the ground.

"Yes, find him, nephew, and bring him here. In fact, if you can manage it, bring Mattie back, too. I want to take her home. I have plenty of quilts, so she'll be snug and warm. Even brought her favorite dress to wear."

Jared nodded. He left the wagon and ventured down the

trail that led to the opening of Mammoth Cave, nicknamed the Wonder of Wonders. He remembered the day he and Uncle Dwight left Mattie here. His uncle clung to her, weeping, even as she patted his shoulder. "Now don't you go fussing, Dwight. I'll be fine and dandy." Jared had to admit a cave seemed a strange place to leave a frail woman. The cave breathed like some living thing. A cool gust of wind blew from within, carrying with it a strange, earthy odor. Jared's breath caught, remembering how Aunt Mattie and others like her were led away into the darkness to some huts built inside. But that doctor was confident the cave would cure them. This must be God's answer to Jared's heartfelt plea. Mattie walked in there sick, but she would come out healed of her affliction. Jared believed it. He had to believe it, even now.

Just then he heard a commotion. Several men appeared from the hotel and headed toward the cave entrance, bearing an empty stretcher and several lanterns. Another man lagged behind and stopped short when he saw Jared.

"You aren't supposed to be here unless you're taking a tour."

"I need to find out about my aunt who is in Dr. Croghan's cave," Jared said to him. "Do you know where the doctor can be found?"

The man grimaced. "Go back to the hotel, and we will let the doctor know you were inquiring."

"But my uncle wishes to see him. He wants to take my aunt home. Her name is Mattie Edwards."

"We will let the doctor know. Now go on."

When they turned their attention away, Jared hastened for a stout tree, ducking behind it to observe the goings-on. The men with flickering lanterns entered the mouth of the cave. The breeze from within blew out several of the lanterns. He waited, wondering what would happen. He rubbed his arms.

His teeth began to chatter. This wasn't from the effects of cold but a growing fear mixed with uncertainty. To him, the cave entrance was like the opening of some gigantic beast, swallowing up the innocent like the huge fish that consumed Jonah. He prayed it had not swallowed up his aunt in death.

For a long time, he waited. Then a new noise erupted from the entrance, startling him. He heard excited voices and then saw the men appear once more, bearing the stretcher. Rubbing his eyes, he stared harder, only to have his stomach lurch. The men carried a white shrouded figure, the face covered by a cloth.

He swallowed hard. His limbs trembled. *Please God, no.* He rushed forward.

"Go back!" they ordered. "You are not to be here!"

"Please, you must tell me who this is. Please, I have to know."

The men paused and looked at each other.

"W–we were told she was very ill," Jared went on, unable to steady his tremulous voice. "Her name is Mattie Edwards. Please tell me if that's her or not."

He saw the glow of recognition in their faces. Then came the nods that confirmed his fear. "Yes. She died this morning. I'm sorry."

Sweat broke out across his brow. He covered his face. What he dreaded most had come to pass.

Aunt Mattie. Dead.

He turned away and stumbled up the path. The tears clouded his vision. How would he ever tell his uncle the terrible news?

❧

Jared gazed upon the ghostlike face of the woman whom he had come to love like a mother. Mattie's final resting place would be the burial ground not far from the Mammoth Hotel. Beside him, loud wails rose from Uncle Dwight. His uncle's grieving began the moment Jared gave the sorrowful news and continued until now, as they looked upon her in a silent state of death. She was dressed in her wedding gown of flowered calico, which Dwight had packed in her trunk. Her hands clasped the few yellow lilies the young lady at the hotel offered. Jared fingered a lone flower from the bouquet given by the woman in the white dress and gazed at its beauty before looking at his aunt one last time.

When the coffin was nailed shut and the burial completed, Uncle Dwight's wails came to an abrupt end. He turned to face Jared. His face grew red. His fists clenched. It began as a mutter within him and then grew to a roar filled with pain.

"You killed her!"

"Uncle?"

"You did it. You're to blame. You killed her just as sure as I'm standing here."

Jared stared in disbelief. "Uncle, please." Tears clouded his eyes. "I loved Aunt Mattie. I would never. . ."

"Y–you made me send her to—to that death cave. You told me I could trust you. You told me that doctor could cure her. Now she's gone! My sweet Mattie is gone forever." He waved his fist, nearly striking him.

"Uncle. . ."

"Get out of my life! I don't ever want to see you again!"

His throat clogged. His stomach rolled into knots. He shook his head, even as Uncle Dwight continued to shout at him. The death knell had sounded, not only for Mattie but also for himself.

He whirled, not knowing what to do. In the distance stood the young woman from the hotel, the one who had given him the flowers. She had witnessed this whole, awful scene unfold in this place of death. Jared caught but a fleeting glimpse of her white dress, so like an angel, before he ran off into the rolling hills.

two

1841—two years earlier

Potato soup and cornbread. Cornbread and potato soup. Susanna watched the soup trickle from her spoon into the bowl of cold watery broth that comprised her main meal. A foot kicked her. She peered underneath to see the feet of her younger brother, stretched to her side of the table. "Stop kicking me, Henry."

"I ain't done nothing," he retorted before his foot slammed into her leg once more.

The elbow of her older brother, Luke, jarred her the next moment, upsetting the spoon. Down the front of her calico ran the watery potato broth, staining her only dress that still looked presentable.

"Luke! How could you! Look at my dress."

"It's just an old dress."

"It was an accident," Mother added. "He didn't mean it."

That was her life these days, one accident after another. Couldn't anyone see how miserable this was? How miserable she was?

Enough was enough. She fled the table, running to her secret place, a rock-laden area by a babbling brook. Many a day she came to sit here and contemplate, to throw her woes into the brook and wish for better times. She picked up a stone and threw it hard into the water. *Why, God?* she wondered, gazing into the leafy branches of the trees. It was difficult enough that she never had any new clothes to wear like her friend Polly at the neighboring farm. But now she had a stain on the only dress that didn't have a hole in it, and from awful potato soup at that. How she longed for pretty dresses of silk, a new bonnet, leather shoes without holes. She wanted something better to eat than cold potato soup and dried cornbread for dinner. She wanted a place where she could eat in peace without having to be bumped and kicked by her brothers. Three times a day they crowded around the tiny table for meals. She could imagine a large home with a separate dining room. The long table would keep her seated far away from her brothers. And she would sit there in a gown of lace all by herself and enjoy every morsel of the fine victuals.

Instead, she was poor, homely, hungry Susanna Barnett in a ratty dress. Susanna threw another stone into the water, watching it disappear. If only her troubles would likewise sink beneath such sweet and refreshing water. If only life could be fair and pleasant instead of harsh and difficult. Day after day, her father tried to make a living from the farm. Day after day, he came home groaning about the rocks, his lazy sons, the mule with a sore in its hoof, and how he wanted to go west with the first wagon trains. "There's nothing here," he complained to Mother. "No food. Can't work the ground. We have no future in Kentucky."

Mother refused even to consider leaving. This was her home, she claimed. Grandma lived in Elizabethtown. Grandpappy was buried here. They had their friends and the little church where they went for services every Sunday. And she hated the thought of traveling so far in a wagon with all the dust, the harsh weather, and the strange Indians.

"But everyone is talking about going out West. The land here is too tired." Papa sat down hard on the stool. "I'm too tired."

They were all weary, so weary they could barely rise to greet the new day. Susanna hoped that one day Mother would wake up and agree to go out West. To her it seemed the answer. She had heard of Oregon Country from neighbors who wanted to follow in the footsteps of a man called Dr. Whitman. He had ventured successfully westward with his wife and now called on others to follow. Once in Oregon Territory, her family could build a large house and raise plenty of food to eat. They would pull out carrots as long as the tines on a pitchfork and potatoes as big as the stones that pitted the Kentucky ground. Game would fill the land in great abundance. A life of paradise in a land of plenty.

Suddenly she heard a terrible sound and horses in distress. She leaped to her feet and whirled about. To her horror, she saw a wagon turned on its side and what appeared to be someone caught underneath, shouting for help. Immediately, Susanna came to the man's side. His face was pinched, his voice scratchy. His red hair reflected the rays of sun. He reached out his hand to her. "Help me, please. My leg is trapped. Get help!"

"I'll get help, sir," she said and raced off to the cabin. "Papa, Papa! There's been an accident. A man is caught under his wagon down the road a piece."

Papa and her brothers wasted no time hightailing it to the wagon and the man caught beneath the jockey seat. In no time, they had the wagon erect. Papa stooped to help the man to a sitting position.

"Oh, my leg," the man groaned, grabbing hold of it. Slowly, he sat back down.

"We'll fetch a doctor," Papa said. "Luke, saddle Honey and go get Doc Hodgens."

"There's no need. I'm a doctor," he managed to say.

"You're a doctor?"

"John Croghan. I–I'm sure you've heard of me. I own the big cave. Mammoth Cave." He then began taking off his shirt and ripping it into strips. "Fetch me some tree limbs, boy," he ordered Luke. "Good stout ones. Not too big but not too small. I don't think my injury is serious. Likely just a sprain, but sometimes you can't tell."

"Don't know if I've heard of that cave," Papa said. "Of course I know there are plenty of caves around."

"I know where one is!" Luke added as he handed the doctor the tree branches and watched him bind the wood to his limb with the strips of cloth. "Do you really own your own cave?"

"Yes, young man, I do. I own the biggest cave in this region—" He finished tying off the makeshift splint with a grunt. He sat back with a sigh. "Largest cave in the world, as a matter of fact."

The questions from Henry and Luke came all at once, like a fleet of arrows loosed upon a target. "Where is it? What does it look like? Where do the passages go? What is there to see?"

"That's enough," Papa said. "Right now we need to get the good doctor somewhere safe. I hope my humble home will do for now."

"Thank you, I'm sure."

Together the brothers and Papa assisted the man to the wagon and guided the horses back to the farm. Susanna followed behind, looking at the man laid out in the back of the wagon with his leg bound by limbs and cloth. Her heart thumped within her. This was no ordinary man who had stumbled upon their farm but someone rich and famous who owned a magnificent cave. It seemed too good to be true. Perhaps even an answer to prayer.

When they had settled the doctor in Luke's bed, the boys

immediately crowded around, asking him all about the cave he owned. Susanna brought the doctor a tin cup of warm milk as he described a wonder of wonders beneath the surface, a place where nothing ever decayed, a place that God Himself etched out of solid rock with His finger. The boys' eyes grew large. They stood fixed in place, never moving an inch, absorbing every word the man said like dry ground beneath a cloudburst.

"I want to go there," Henry declared.

"I'd like to live in a place like that," Luke added.

Dr. Croghan chuckled, sipping on the milk. "If you're going to live there, you'll still have to grow your food in the outside world. You could build yourselves small cottages inside the cave, I suppose. It's certainly big enough. I once even considered putting a library inside the cave myself. How great it would be to study in such magnificence." He grew quiet then. "But it's very dark in the cave. Black as night. Damp. You can hear the water trickling. But it stays a constant temperature."

"I'd grow my corn outside and bring it in," Luke decided. "And use plenty of lanterns."

"Can't grow crops nowhere around here," Papa said thoughtfully. "In fact, one can hardly grow a kernel of corn in this ground. The ground grows rocks instead. And then the ground looks like it's sinking away in these parts. Kentucky is only for the starving."

"We aren't starving," Mother said, her hands flying to her hips. "And don't you go using it as an excuse to leave either, Hiram. That's all anyone around these parts talks about. Leaving and going elsewhere. Like there isn't anything here worth living for."

"There is, I must say," said the good doctor. "If you could see the cave you would think differently about Kentucky. I remember when Archie first showed it to me. I was amazed. It's a place of refuge. Maybe even a place of healing. I've been studying the possibility. There are caves in Europe where doctors allow invalids to live in them, and they've had excellent results."

"But a cave won't get us the food we need," Papa added glumly.

Susanna looked at the wooden plank flooring of the cabin beneath the shabby shoes she wore. Could there really be something like a cave existing under their house? It seemed so strange to her, like a story she might have heard told by an old farmer smoking his corncob pipe and telling tall tales to his cronies. A huge cave, big enough to live in. An underground castle with rocky engravings like paintings on the walls. This couldn't be a mere story told by the doctor for their amusement. It must be real.

Several days passed before the doctor proclaimed himself much improved and healthy enough to travel back to his cave where he could finish recuperating. In the meantime, the boys had all but exhausted the man who told them tales of adventures conducted by his servant, Stephen Bishop, the one who mapped out the cave. When Papa came forward to present the doctor with some crutches he had made, a smile spread across Dr. Croghan's face.

"Now I would like to do something for you all," he announced, sizing up each of them.

"There is no need," Mother said. "We are only doing the Christian thing by helping a neighbor in need."

"But I want to. How would you like to work for me?"

One by one their eyes grew large in astonishment. "Work for you?" Papa repeated. "But we know nothing about caves."

"I could use some help. I own a hotel, you see, near the

entrance to the cave. I would like to run tours. And I'd like to have you come live at the hotel and help the visitors who come to the hotel for tours of the cave. Archie does most of the managing of the place, but he could use the help. And we expect quite a few visitors to come with the fine summer weather soon upon us."

Papa looked at Mother. The boys immediately latched onto them, tugging, pleading with them to say yes. Susanna could only stand there dumbfounded.

"We don't know anything about caves. . . ," Papa said once more.

"There isn't much to know, really. You don't need to lead a tour or anything. I have guides who do that. I just need a nice family with smiles on their faces, who would greet the visitors and make them feel at ease. You all seem perfect for such work."

Papa exchanged glances with Mother. "I don't know. Me and the missus will have to talk it over."

"Of course. When you come to a decision you can send word to me by way of the general store in Brownsville. But I do hope you will consider it. There's such great enthusiasm here. I believe it's the very thing I need to make my cave a success."

Watching the man slowly mount the wagon seat and wave good-bye, Papa stood next to Mother. "What do you think, Matilda?"

"I don't think we should abandon the beautiful land and farm the good Lord gave to us," she retorted. "And that's that."

❧

1843—Present Day

Susanna glanced about the new land God had seen fit to give them as temporary keepers. There were rolling hills with the beginnings of spring wildflowers abloom, trees, the long muddy road that brought in the carriages, and the wooden buildings strung together that comprised the hotel and residences for the visitors. And, of course, the strange aura emanating from that famous hole of Dr. Croghan's known as Mammoth Cave. Two years had passed since the day of the wagon accident when Dr. Croghan injured himself. Now, Susanna never felt more content. All her dreams had come true when they accepted the work here and took charge of the tours that left the hotel several times a day to see the famous cave. Mother had said all along that God was looking out for them, and now Susanna believed it with all her heart. Standing in the large bedroom she had all to herself and looking at her rich silk gown, her feet clad in new shoes, she knew God had been good to her family. He had seen their poverty and had brought the wealthy Dr. Croghan to their doorstep in their time of need. Not that she would have wished him or anyone injured for her family's well being. But God had providentially used the man to set their feet on a path of prosperity—and when they might have starved if they had remained on the farm. All things had surely worked together for good for them that love the Lord, just as Mother had often read from the big black Bible.

Susanna gazed about her room. How she loved this hotel. The fine furniture. Good solid wood floors. A ballroom. A library filled with books. The wonderful food served three times a day that included many kinds of vegetables, real sourdough bread, chicken and pork, cookies and teacakes. And a huge table at which to dine, where her brothers sat on the opposite end, well away from her. Mammoth Hotel had been a glimpse of heaven—until she met Jared Edwards.

For two years, she had been shielded from life, it seemed.

The hardship, the pain, even death. Then death suddenly came calling one dreadful day—and in Dr. Croghan's famous cave, of all places. Now, death overshadowed everything.

Susanna learned of Jared's name from the papers Dr. Croghan had in his possession concerning the treatment of Jared's aunt, Mattie Edwards. The woman's death had opened Susanna's eyes. No one was supposed to die here. This was a miracle cave, after all. A cave God had made, as the good doctor had said. A cave that could heal as well as stir up excitement far and wide. But something had gone terribly wrong.

Susanna was one of the first to learn something was amiss when one of the doctor's assistants came running to the hotel, claiming an invalid had died in the cave that morning. Susanna could hardly believe it. She, like everyone else, thought the cave to be the perfect place for the sick to recover. It was an area wrought out of stone and filled with moisture-laden air, a place vastly different from anything that existed in the outside world. Upon hearing about it, people flocked to the cave in the hopes of finding a cure for their loved ones sickened by the consumption. Now, most tragically, someone had died. And to her dismay, it was the relative of the young man who had pulled up in the wagon with the woman's husband beside him, asking to see the doctor. The young man named Jared Edwards.

When the assistants brought out the woman's body, wrapped in a sheet, the older man broke into terrible wails that sent shivers racing through Susanna. She'd never seen or heard anyone so distraught. During the burial the older man fell to his knees, clawing at the dead woman, pleading with her to wake up and come home. And in the background stood Jared with his head hanging low, twisting his hat in his hands, his lips moving in prayer. The sorrow lay thick and heavy around him. It was an awful sight to see. Moved by it all, Susanna did what she could. She gathered what flowers were growing that early in March, some wild trout lilies, and gave the bouquet to him. He took them, his dark eyes meeting hers, his lips forming the silent words of *thank you.*

And then, she witnessed the scene that still remained fixed in her mind. Awful accusations spilled forth from the uncle as he blamed Jared for the woman's death. Then, in a booming voice, the uncle ordered Jared out of his life. She watched with a heavy heart as the young man ran off and never looked back.

Susanna decided to follow Jared. She wanted to comfort him, to tell him everything would be all right, to show him that someone cared. However, he was too strong and quick, racing through the woods like a fine steed and disappearing over a rise. She slowed to a walk and finally stopped. Her heart beat rapidly, her breath came fast and furious, but her spirit sank. How could this have happened? The cave was supposed to be a place of hope—the same hope that helped her family out of their poverty. Instead, it had become a place of death for Jared and a place that drove him apart from his uncle. His hope had been dashed upon the very rocks meant to heal.

Slowly she made her way back to the hotel, the cheerfulness that once permeated her life vanquished by what she had witnessed. In front of the hotel, Dr. Croghan was conferring with Papa over what happened. The grim expressions were clearly visible on their faces.

"I want men to stand guard over the premises," Croghan told Papa. "I don't trust that man who lost his wife. He seemed quite distraught."

"I'm sure it will pass, Doctor. Life and death are in the hands of the Lord."

"Even so, I want the hotel and the cave entrance guarded. We are the law in this place, and I will not tolerate lawlessness." Dr. Croghan shook his head and returned to the cave to see after the surviving invalids.

Papa sighed, only to straighten when he caught sight of Susanna. "And where did you run off to, daughter?"

"I was following the young man who lost his aunt in the cave."

"Why? There is nothing more we can do."

"There must be, Papa. The doctor promised the people who came to his cave that they would get better. And that man was. . ." She dared not say how his grief had moved her in ways she didn't think possible.

"The doctor promised nothing of the sort. His prayer was, of course, that the people would get well. Nevertheless, not all have the strength to endure the treatment in the cave. Dr. Croghan made sure the invalids and their families knew this."

Her gaze traveled to the place of distress, that dark hole, recalling the cold air rising up from the entrance in the summer. Many times the blast of air beckoned to her on a hot August day to come inside and cool off. She had never yet yielded to the temptation. Papa and her brothers had toured the inside of the cave and marveled over it. She had never seen it, nor was she certain she wanted to now—after what happened.

"There is nothing we can do," Papa said again. "We have business to attend. Please make sure the guests are assembled and ready for the next tour."

Susanna looked at her father in alarm. "Don't you think we should cancel the tours for today? Someone just died, Papa. We should be in mourning."

A look of irritation filled his rough face. He adjusted the hat he wore. "Dr. Croghan didn't give us orders to stop the tours. We're getting paid to organize them. So we will go on as if nothing happened." He stepped closer. "And you are not to tell anyone about this either. I don't want the guests fearful. This is our work, daughter. This is how we live. Life goes on. So smile and be cheerful."

When he turned and walked away, a great sadness filled her. No one would even pause to mourn the dead. It was only tours and money, work and duty.

Cornbread and potatoes. Potatoes and cornbread.

She winced. *I am no better. I love this new life as much as anyone. God, please help me trust in Your will and not my own wants and desires. Help me know what is right and good in Your eyes alone.*

three

"Go away!" A door opened. The muzzle of a gun poked out, gleaming in the sun's rays. "I'm warning you. Not another step."

Jared walked tentatively into the yard. It had been awhile since he had been back. He'd stayed away, in his cabin, thinking and praying about his circumstances, giving them each some time alone. Suddenly he caught sight of his uncle's rifle.

"Uncle Dwight, it's me."

"I know who it is. Don't make me use my gun now. Go away!"

"Please, can we talk? We need to talk about this."

"I have nothing more to say to you. Go away!"

"Uncle, I. . ."

The gun fired. Jared jumped as a bullet whizzed by him and lodged in the wooden fencing behind him. A chill swept over him.

Uncle Dwight, visibly shaken, lowered his weapon. "I didn't mean to do that. It was an accident. Please, just leave me alone."

Jared needed no further urging, not after feeling the breeze of a bullet brush by him. He took to his heels, racing by his uncle's fields, which Jared had started to plow before all this happened. Past the fields, he pressed onward into the woods where spring plants were emerging from the cold ground. He paused to catch his breath, looking to see if his uncle had followed. Through the naked tree branches, he saw the faint curl of smoke rising out of the cabin's chimney. He could see the man's rage as he stood in the doorway of the humble log home, waving his fist and shouting. The hard voice echoed in the glade. *Go away! And never come back!*

Jared sank to the hard ground. How could this have happened? *Why, God?* He scooped some clay from the ground and formed it into a ball. Pitching it against a stout tree, he watched the clod hit, then break apart. Just like his life. He had hardly eaten or slept since that terrible day at Mammoth Cave when they buried his aunt. In fact, this was the first time he had mustered the courage to visit his uncle, hoping the tide of grief had passed and reconciliation might be in his grasp. He had never been more wrong, he realized, as the faint smell of gunpowder reached his nostrils. Nothing had changed. The anger, the hurt, the pain was ever alive, even more so now than before. He had no idea what to do about it, either.

Just then, he heard the rustle of fragile bushes. Footsteps crunched through the downed leaves left from last autumn. Fear rose up in his throat. He began to inch himself away, behind a tree trunk that he prayed would offer him some protection. His heart began to race. He wiped the sweat from his brow.

Uncle Dwight appeared from behind the trees, his boots covered in mud, his face swathed in anger. At least he didn't carry the gun. "What do you want here, Jared?" he sputtered. "You sneaking around my place all the time, up to no good." He rubbed his face.

Jared was thankful to find his uncle talking to him. "I miss you, Uncle. We need each other. The fields need plowing. We need to get the crops planted soon."

"I don't need you no more. I trusted you. I trusted you with my Mattie. You told me to take her to the place and leave her in a pit of stone. And look what happened. She's gone. Gone forever, buried in the cold ground. She went into some cold ground and never came out again." He began to cough.

"Uncle, please believe me. If I had known any of this would happen, I'd never have considered sending her there. I loved her, too. I never would have put her life in danger. I wanted to save her life."

His uncle stood there, rubbing his face. He looked tired, worn out, frail, and fragile, like a dying tree ready to fall if hit by a breath of wind. "You just don't know anything about love, Jared. You don't know what it means to have the love of a good woman—someone to care for and someone who cares about you, standing by your side. You don't know what we had, your aunt and I, and what you stole. Now I want you to go away and leave me alone."

The look on his uncle's face sealed it. Jared could say no more. He took to his feet and walked deeper into the woods, away from his uncle's grief, headed for the road. He paused. Where would he go? He refused to return to his cabin right now. There was nothing for him there. It was a cold and lonely place. Whenever he saw the tablecloth his aunt had made or the flower the young woman had given him at the burial, lying in the Bible all withered, his throat ached. Great heaves filled him. Why was he blamed for this? His uncle should blame the people who had done this to Mattie, that doctor who had made all those fancy promises and then broke every one of them. The doctor who had sentenced Mattie to death by his impressive words of healing and miracles. Tears clouded his eyes. He had believed in the miracle, and the miracle had failed him.

He walked along, kicking up the ground as he pondered his uncle's words. No, he didn't know the love of woman. Maybe he needed to. Maybe a woman's love would help him understand his uncle's hurt and help redirect his life. For some reason, he thought of the young and pretty woman at the hotel. He didn't even know her name, but he remembered her very well—the white dress, the small bouquet of spring flowers she had given him for his aunt's burial, the solemn vigil she had kept during the service. He looked often at the flower pressed inside the only book he owned, his Bible. Her fine dress of pure white reminded him of freshly fallen snow and illustrated her rich status. Why would he even consider her as someone who might introduce him to the kind of love his uncle described? How could he think she would so much as give him a second glance? She didn't know any more about him than he knew about her. She was wealthy, without a care in the world. He was only a farmer caught up in a spiral of grief and uncertainty. But he did desperately want to know what it meant to care for someone, to have a marriage like his uncle and his aunt had known, to understand Uncle Dwight and maybe himself.

Jared returned to his cabin and saddled his tar-colored horse. He decided he wanted to take another look. Not at the death cave or the fancy hotel, but at the woman who'd been thoughtful enough to be there for him in the saddest of times. He wanted to know her name. Where she came from. Who she was. Why she cared.

He took off down the dusty road. It was a fair piece to the hotel. Along the way, he passed wagonloads of patrons traveling to and from the cave. He didn't know how he would gain the young lady's attention. Maybe he could just be a shadow among the many visitors, a silent observer as she had been, quiet and thoughtful, perhaps even prayerful. Maybe she would be as attracted to him as he was to her. On the other hand, maybe he was being downright foolish to even think she could fulfill the role of which his uncle spoke.

"Whoa, there! Whoa!"

Jared hadn't even seen the horse and rider barreling toward him. He pulled at the reins to slow his mount, guiding it off the road.

"Hey, you'd better look where yer going! I plum near ran you over."

"Sorry about that."

The rider peered down at him. "You look familiar. You Dwight Edwards's nephew by chance?"

"Yes, I am. Jared Edwards."

"I'm George Higgins. Heard about your aunt. Sorry. Death has struck again, it seems. Some kind of curse in that cave, that's what it is. I just come from there myself."

Jared shielded his eyes from the sun's glare. "What do you mean?"

"I lost my cousin in Croghan's cave. He died the day before yesterday. Now I'm heading over to talk to your uncle. I want to know what we can do about this."

Someone else had died in the cave? Thoughts of the young woman vanished upon hearing this news. While Jared realized he should mourn the man's loss, he wrestled with a sense of relief. Someone else shared in the grief, the confusion, and the pain. Someone else had trusted in this Dr. Croghan and found their loved one taken away. He was not alone.

"Where are you headed?" the man asked. "Not back to that cave?"

"Uh." He panicked. "I, uh." He didn't dare tell him what

he was up to. . .how he was seeking the woman who worked there.

"Come on and ride with me to your uncle's."

Jared shook his head. "We're not on speaking terms after my aunt passed away. Uncle Dwight blames me for it. I convinced him to take Mattie there, you see—to let that doctor cure her. Now he hates me for it."

"I'm sorry to hear that. I understand, though. My son Riley don't say much to me neither. Well, we can't let this get to us. We gotta come together and see what can be done. Can't let no rich doctor come up with some kinda no-good idea that takes away our loved ones. I miss my cousin something awful. He and I, we went fishing there in the river all the time. I sure do miss him."

"Did your cousin have the consumption?"

"Yes, and he insisted the doctor could heal him in that fancy cave of his. Said how the air there could do wonders. I tried to talk him out of it. Told him he needed to go somewhere warm, like the Carolinas. But he just sat there, skin and bones he was, and said, 'George, I don't have long to live in this world. If the good Lord gave us this cave as some miracle, then I'd be a fool not to try it.' And I believed him." He paused, his face darkening as if storm clouds had drifted across it. "Now I wonder who's the real fool?"

Jared had been told he was the fool for taking his aunt there. But there must be more to this than what he could see with his own eyes. Surely God could make something good come out of this—maybe by bringing people into his life, people he never would have met otherwise. "So, what do you think we should do?"

"I'll tell you one thing. I'm gonna find out what that doctor's gonna do about this."

"Nothing we say or do is going to bring back our loved ones," Jared said.

"You're right about that. But we can do something so's no one else dies. In my mind, he ought to close down that place. Seal that cave up. Keep everyone out of it. It's a death cave now. No more grand Mammoth Cave, no siree. We're gonna put a stop to it somehow. Think your uncle might be willing to help?"

The idea of building a bridge to his uncle's affections, a way to span the chasm that kept them apart, appealed to Jared like no other. With his own family gone, he had no one else. Just the thought of reconciliation made his heart leap. "I'm sure he would. He misses Aunt Mattie. I think he would do anything to make sure no one else suffers like he has."

"That's it, then. I'll see who we can get to go talk to that doctor as soon as possible. And we're gonna make such a noisy fuss, they won't be able to do anything else but close that cave." He tipped his hat. "I'll put in a good word for you to your uncle. Make no mistake."

"Much obliged." He was glad to see someone willing to break through the storminess in his life. Maybe a rainbow was about to appear, a promise of something new, a hope for the future.

❧

Back inside his cabin that night, sleep eluded Jared. He tried to rest but soon got up and started a fire in the fireplace. He was hungry and decided to make some biscuits. He hadn't been hungry these days and often skipped meals, but tonight he would make biscuits in honor of his aunt. She often told him that a young man should be able to do his own cooking—especially once he got married and the woman was tending to the younguns—but even before that. He could still envision the gentle form of his aunt in front of the fireplace, showing him how to bake biscuits in the Dutch oven over a bed of glimmering coals. Then came her recipe for apple pan dowdy. Corn pone. Flapjacks. Sourdough bread. He ate well on the heels of her tutoring. That is, until the dark day when his appetite vanished into the bowels of the earth along with Mattie.

He set to work making the biscuits and spooning the dough into the Dutch oven. He then opened the cabin door for a breath of air. It was a cold night. He saw something dart by in the air. Then another. Bats. They were frequent visitors with all the caves in the area. He didn't like them. They were too swift and mysterious, nearly invisible. At least he didn't feel the night itself mysterious and without hope. In fact, he felt better tonight than he had in a long time, as if hope had been restored. Jared had prayed all evening that this man named Higgins could get through to Uncle Dwight and make him see that Jared wasn't the enemy. Afterwards, Higgins stopped by his place as he was putting up the stock to tell him the meeting with his uncle went well. Uncle Dwight and Higgins got along famously, and in the end, they agreed to confront the doctor at the hotel. Maybe on the heels of this meeting, healing and forgiveness would soon follow. Both Mattie and this fractured relationship with his uncle could finally be laid to rest.

For Jared's part, he told Higgins he would try to help, perhaps by convincing the young woman at the hotel to intervene in their circumstance. She had been there at his aunt's burial. He felt certain she would help. There was something different about her, something unlike the others in that place. For one thing, she cared. She had a semblance of mercy. She must be sympathetic to the agony of death to be there at some stranger's burial. She wouldn't have given him the flowers for his aunt's grave or stood by in silent reverence otherwise. Jared intended to appeal to her merciful heart.

He returned to check on the biscuits. Maybe out of all this, good would come. God would knit him with a woman who would teach him about love and life—such as his Aunt Mattie had shown until death snatched her away. Maybe it would make him appreciate life more. Maybe he wouldn't feel so lonely either. He would finally have a purpose.

He turned the biscuits over one by one. They were browning nicely. There were good changes coming, like the deep red of a sunset signaling fair weather. For the first time since his aunt's passing, hope filled his heart.

four

A golden glow formed on the distant horizon with the first rays of sun awakening the new dawn. Susanna arose from her bed and stretched her arms. A knock sounded at the door. She answered it to find Martha, bringing linen towels and fresh water in a porcelain pitcher.

"Good morning, Martha," Susanna chirped. For some reason, she felt happy and carefree today. Perhaps it had to do with the delightful dream she'd had of strolling through the woods beyond the hotel and encountering a handsome man on horseback. He had tipped his hat to her like a true gentleman. He asked if she cared to ride with him on his black steed—an offer she hastened to accept. He offered his stout hand to help her astride the animal. They rode fast and furious through the tall grass and into the Kentucky woods filled with flowers all in bloom. Susanna could still feel the wind in her hair and hear her laughter.

"Miss?" Martha asked, her face as rigid as stone with nary a smile to be found.

Susanna sent her a quizzical look before turning to dip her hands in the cold water, splashing it onto her face. She patted her face dry with the towel Martha offered. "I do hope we are having a wonderful breakfast. I'm starving."

"Eggs and ham, Miss. Yankee dough cakes. Applesauce."

"How grand." Susanna grew hungry just listening to it all. None of the hateful potato soup and cornbread could be found here except for an occasional corn pudding or fancy potato dish.

She hummed a tune as she began the lengthy task of dressing for the day. There were the long, itchy stockings held up by garters. Drawers separated at the waist. A linen chemise. Several stiff starched petticoats, one on top of the other. A corset, which Martha helped to tie. Then a dress with a tight-fitting bodice fastened with hooks and eyes. The skirt arced in a fashionable style, taking on the shape of a bell from the many petticoats underneath. She sighed in satisfaction at her image in the mirror. Perfect for her man on his black horse, if only he would come. She began to twirl around the room, feeling giddy and a bit light-headed. *I am a fine lady at last.* How she dreamed of this while sitting by the brook, dressed in ugly calico stained by Luke's clumsiness. Soon there would be no end to the suitors who would arrive, asking permission to court her.

"Susanna!" Mother said from the doorway. "Please contain yourself. You're a lady, after all."

"But today I will be whisked away by a handsome stranger on a horse darker than even that cave," she said with a giggle.

Mother shook her head. "I don't know where you come up with these ideas of yours. Hurry now. Breakfast is being served. Your brothers are already seated. And we have guests."

Susanna took a brush to her hair and quickly wound it in a knot at the nape of her neck, fastening it into place with combs. Curly ringlets graced each cheek flushed with excitement. "Do you think it will be busy at the cave today now that pleasant weather has come?"

"Every day is busy. Since the tourists now arrive at the hotel by stage, there is never a day it isn't. Everyone is curious. And yes, I do believe the warmer weather brings more people."

Susanna took one more look at her appearance before following her mother to the dining area. Several guests were seated at the large table along with her family, some of whom she didn't know. She offered a greeting and took a seat.

"The day is already half gone," Luke teased. "Where have you been?"

"I was having a wonderful dream, if it's any of your concern."

"She dreams of riding in a fine carriage," Henry added with a smirk.

Susanna held her head high. "As a matter of fact, I did dream of a noble on his black steed who will carry me away to a grand palace on a hill." She unfolded the napkin across her lap and waited expectedly for breakfast to be served on pewter platters.

The brothers hooted until Papa and Mother glared at them, silencing the rowdiness. "You would do well to remember yourselves," Mother said. "We have guests."

Only then did Susanna pay notice to the three men at the table, dressed in their stiff coats, staring at her family. She recognized Mr. Archibald Miller, who managed the hotel, along with two business associates of Dr. Croghan's, though the doctor himself was not present.

"He is caring for the invalids," Mr. Miller responded when asked of the doctor's whereabouts. He helped himself to a large serving of ham.

"I hear another invalid died during the night," said a man who introduced himself as Mr. Witherspoon.

All the giddiness Susanna felt that morning suddenly disappeared. "Another one died?" she said before clamping her lips shut, remembering her station.

"That makes three," Mr. Miller went on, eating ravenously, as if the news only heightened his appetite. "The doctor isn't certain what to think."

"It appears to me this grand experiment of his is on the

brink of failure," said Mr. Witherspoon. "I, for one, feel the cottages inside the cave should be closed immediately."

"Let's not be so hasty," another man ventured—a Mr. Grimes, with thinning hair and spectacles, who some said wanted to take over the hotel from Dr. Croghan so the doctor could concentrate on caring for the invalids. "No one knows how sick they were before they entered the cave. It may be that only a miracle from the Most High could have saved them."

"I'm concerned about this news reaching the tourists," Papa added. "We don't want people fearful of going into the cave. It will decrease business. And we depend on visitors for their money."

"But we are talking about people's lives," said Mr. Witherspoon. "They are worth more than money, are they not?"

Papa flushed. "Of course. I meant nothing to the contrary."

Yes, you did, Papa, Susanna thought. *That's all you think about. I hear you and Luke talking. You're always asking how to bring more tourists to the cave, how to convince them to spend their money on the tours and stay at the hotel.* She looked down at her brown silk brocade dress. But if they did not make the money, how would she buy a new bonnet? A gossamer silk dress with rosettes across the neckline for a grand ball or any of the other fashions she had seen in the Godey's Lady's book? Yet she could not ignore the other side of this issue, which she had witnessed that one day—a day filled with grief that still sprung up in her heart, of the man named Jared who had lost his aunt, and then the chastisement he received as if it were his fault.

"I agree that we do have a business to run," said Mr. Miller. "If we must close the underground cottages to preserve the cave and what it gives the visitors, then so be it. The tours can still proceed."

"And what of the invalids in residence?" asked Mr. Grimes. "Where will they go?"

"They can go elsewhere. There are many places for them to recuperate in the South. But surely we cannot allow this to interfere with what we are doing here."

"And what exactly are we doing?" Susanna piped up. "Besides seeing poor people suffer and die and others grieve while our pockets fill with money?"

Papa put down his fork, aghast. Mother stared and shook her head. "Susanna, hush up! Remember yourself."

Susanna ignored her. "I hear what you gentlemen are saying. But is that all we are here to do? Make money?"

"You see?" Mr. Witherspoon said, pointing his fork at Susanna. "The young lady here knows that a gift of God shouldn't turn us into stone. We must think of other ways to use it for the good of mankind and not simply for greed's sake."

No one answered for a time. The eggs and ham grew quite cold on the plates.

Luke finally stood to his feet. "I will tell you how it has been used for good. The cave helped our family out of a pit of poverty and put our feet on firm ground. And I, for one, don't ever intend to go back to that kind of living again."

Stillness fell over the table before everyone returned their attention to the food. Susanna looked down at her dress, remembering that time of poverty, the rags she had worn, the soup and cornbread that comprised her sustenance. But were her present luxuries worth the uneasiness she felt?

❧

"That was utterly delightful! Though I fear my shoes will never be the same."

"Amazing," another remarked, removing the dusty cave costume worn by the visitors to protect their fine garments from the dirt and mud that abounded in the cave. "How wonderful that we can go and see such wonders right beneath our feet. The Gothic Chapel. The Star Chamber. Washington's Dome."

Susanna was used to such exclamations from visitors who came out of the cave as they described the features they had seen. It seemed strange that she had not witnessed such wonders for herself. Her father had seen them. So had her brothers. But she hadn't, nor had her mother. Though women did go on the tours, Mother felt it unseemly for Susanna to venture into such strange and dark places. And now, with the invalids living there the past few months, she had no desire to enter it. Yet the stories still proved intriguing. And hearing them for two years now, she felt as if she knew the cave anyway, despite having never seen the inside of it for herself.

"But I did not like seeing the sickly ones," said the first woman, dabbing her face with a handkerchief. "The guide should have taken us on a different route rather than by the dreary cottages. Most dreadful to be in such a terrible state."

Word soon came that yet another invalid had succumbed to the effects of the treatment. Rumors among the staff grew—wondering what Dr. Croghan would do with the sick, and what might become of the cave now that four invalids had died. At least from what Susanna could observe, the news of the deaths did not seem to stop the curious. They still arrived daily by stage and wagon, their faces expectant, willing to pay the necessary fee for either the short or long tours.

"I looked away," said the friend. "How could I not? The dreadful sight made me so afraid."

"Goodness, Margaret. There is nothing to fear. They are but poor, suffering souls. More dead than alive, I must say. I wonder if anything can be done for them?"

"I think they should leave. There are hardly any of them left. Moreover, the cave is so dark and filled with smoke. How one can live in such a place. . .I don't understand."

Susanna remained preoccupied by the ladies' conversation, even as she tried to help a couple buy tickets for the tour. The ladies soon left to partake of the refreshments served after the tour was completed—hot tea and biscuits with plenty of jam. However, Susanna couldn't help but think of the sickness and the people who seemed to get no better, despite the doctor's best intentions to cure them. It seemed a curse loomed in the deep.

"I say, when does the next tour leave, young lady?"

Susanna shook her head and gazed into the eyes of a gentleman dressed in his fine frock coat and high collar. He leaned on an elaborately carved cane. "In about ten minutes, sir. If you would wait in the front parlor for the guides, they will escort you to the cavern entrance. And there are costumes, as well, to put on if you wish to protect your clothing."

He gave a huff and left, mumbling about her inattentiveness and the sorry state of this hotel's staff.

"Are you dreaming again, sister?"

Susanna glanced about to find Luke standing there, holding several lanterns, and ready to hand them to the guides for the tour. "Luke, did you hear the news? Another invalid died in the cave."

He shrugged. "There is nothing that can be done, Susanna. It's not our affair, after all. We are here to help the visitors." He pulled a watch out of his vest pocket. "Please tell the visitors to gather in the hall so we might proceed. The guides are ready." His eyes narrowed. "And don't concern yourself with things you can't change."

Susanna sighed. How could he be so unfeeling? The one who had died belonged to someone dear, like the young man

Jared who had lost his aunt. Could they not pause for just a moment and grieve? Or must they only do the tours without a thought given to the one who had left this world or for those who endured such loss? Mother and Papa would both reprimand her if they knew her thoughts, saying she dwelled too much on the whole affair. They would tell her that life and death were a part of this world. She must concentrate on her work and not let it affect her. If only she could. Maybe if she hadn't gathered the flowers for that Jared fellow. Maybe if she hadn't witnessed the pain in his eyes or heard the wail and chastisement of the older man who drove Jared out of his life. How does one forget that kind of pain?

Susanna returned to the drawing room to see if there were any others interested in the final tour of the day, when Luke came running back. "Where's Papa?"

"I don't know. What's the matter?"

"There's trouble afoot! Quick, we must find him."

Susanna hastened for the living areas to find Mother mending a blouse. "Mother, Luke says there's trouble. Do you know where Papa can be found?"

"No, I don't. What kind of trouble?"

All at once, she heard shouts from outside. She ran for the window and peered out. Fear gripped her spirit. A party of riders on horseback had descended on the hotel. A brownish cloud arose from the many hooves plodding the dry ground.

"Oh no!" Mother whispered. "What shall we do?"

Susanna hastened for the door, even as Mother pleaded with her to stay. She came to the part of the hotel and the drawing room where the visitors sat huddled together, their eyes wide with fright. "What is happening?" they asked her at once.

"I don't know. Please stay here inside the hotel until we find out."

She slipped out of the room and through a side entrance to meet a burly man dismounting from his horse. He demanded that Mr. Miller send for Dr. Croghan. Papa was there as well as Luke, trying in vain to calm the irate man.

"He is in the underground cottages helping the invalids," Mr. Miller told the man. "He should be back presently."

"He's not helping anyone!" another man shouted. "That cave is a place of death. Now you get him right now, or we're going in there after him."

Susanna stared at the man cradling the long barrel of a rifle. She managed to cover her mouth before a startled cry escaped. Upon the order from Mr. Miller, Luke raced down the steep hill toward the mouth of the cave to find Dr. Croghan. Many agonizing moments slipped by as the men stood before the hotel, their faces encased in hostile looks. Luke finally appeared with the doctor, who came running up the hill accompanied by several assistants.

"What seems to be the trouble?" asked Dr. Croghan.

"Plenty of trouble," barked the man with the gun. "You killed my Mattie."

"And my cousin, Charles," said another, "in that cave you think helps the sick. They only die in there."

"What are you going to do about it?" shouted a third man. A fourth nodded his head in agreement. The men began to pace about, their faces filled with wrath.

Dr. Croghan lifted his hands. "Please, gentlemen. Let us remain calm. As you know, when you entrusted your loved ones in my care, there was no promise that they would be made well. Many came here quite ill already and perhaps beyond help. But I did my best, and I am happy to say that some are indeed recovering."

The man with the gun stepped forward. "So you're telling

me my Mattie didn't have to come here, that she was going to die anyway in your cave? That there weren't no hope?"

"Sir, I'm terribly sorry for your loss. We have done everything to care for them. But as I said, some did not adapt well to the cave's environment. And it may be that your wife was one of the few."

The man shook with rage, even as Susanna watched a younger man step up to try to calm him down. She sucked in her breath. The young man was Jared Edwards. She was certain of it. Their eyes met for the first time since that terrible day when he buried his aunt in the cemetery not far from the hotel. She saw him step back, his gaze never leaving her. Fear gnawed at her. Why was he looking at her that way?

The man then slipped around the crowd of people. She retreated into the dusk, wishing she had listened to Mother and stayed inside the hotel. He was coming toward her, walking at a brisk step, his face set in determination. Gasping, Susanna hastened for the nearest door and safety.

"Please wait!" he called to her.

Something in his voice made her stop—a pleading she could not ignore.

"I need to talk to you."

She tried to settle her nervous tremors, praying she was not about to face some hostile man wishing revenge. "Please, if you have questions, talk to Dr. Croghan. It's his cave, after all. I have nothing to do with it."

"Yes, you do. You have everything to do with it. You may be the only one who can help me. You did once before when no one else cared. I know you care. I saw it with my own eyes."

She looked at him, curious at the words he spoke. "I don't know what you mean."

"The day my aunt died. The flowers you gave me. The way

you stood there, watching, listening." He stepped forward, planting his hands inside the pockets of his pants. "I never thanked you for it."

Susanna stood still, unsure of what to say.

"I can tell you care," he went on. "You're not like the others in this place."

"You're wrong. We all care here, very much. The doctor, my family. . ."

"But I believe you care enough to do what needs to be done."

She didn't like the connotation behind his words. "What is it I'm supposed to do?"

He looked around. "Is there a place we can talk?"

Susanna showed him to a wooden bench, one of many that lined the pathways in the area. In the background, she could still hear the raised voices of the men challenging the doctor and see the glow of lanterns illuminating the twilight. "I fear those men might hurt the doctor and my papa," she said quickly. "Your uncle looks ready to use that gun of his."

"He's very sad," Jared agreed, kicking a foot into the dirt. "All of them are. But they don't want to hurt anyone. They know the cave is dangerous and want something done about it. You've seen it for yourself, I'm sure."

"I've never seen inside it."

He looked up with wide eyes as if surprised by this news. "But you know that people have died in it. That it's not safe."

Susanna didn't know how to respond. She never thought of the cave as dangerous, only dark and mysterious, but a miracle of God's creation just the same. How can His creation be dangerous? "It isn't a danger. Dr. Croghan only wishes to help people. Like he said, perhaps some came too sick to be helped by his methods. But that doesn't make the cave dangerous."

He stared, unblinking. "I had hoped you, out of all the people here, would see how this place brings nothing but death. That you would help me convince this doctor to close down Mammoth Cave before others suffer."

She stared, shocked that he would even ask her such a thing. She stood to her feet in haste. "I can't do that!"

"Why not?"

"The cave is God's creation. His world beneath the ground. And I believe He wants us to see it, or He wouldn't have made it."

"But He never meant it to be used by others for evil, did He? Or to have people die in it? His creations are intended for good."

The words struck her with such force, she took a step back. All the breath left her. She gasped. "This is not an evil place, and we are not evil people. I don't know how you can say such things. Good night."

She stumbled away, back to the safety of the hotel, with Jared's words stinging her heart. She sat in a chair, trying to make sense out of all this, when Luke and her father returned, red faced and tremulous.

"Dr. Croghan managed the situation well," Papa said, accepting the cup of tea a servant hastily brought to him. "I think the force we showed also helped, having armed men at our call. We will not be intimated."

"They'll be back, Papa," Luke said. "It's only a matter of time."

Susanna looked down at her shaking hands, thinking of Jared and how he had called them all evil. It made her shudder. If only they had stopped to grieve for those who were lost. Maybe none of this would have happened.

five

For days afterwards, Jared's words haunted Susanna. She recalled his presence as he sat beside her on the bench—recollected his every detail, even down to the woodsy scent his clothes carried. Most of all, when she thought of Jared, she envisioned his determination to see things made right after the loss he had suffered. At night, she dreamed of the people in the cave with their peaked faces, dressed in white garments, their hands reaching out to her. *Help us! You're the only one who can help us! The doctor has us locked in this cave. It's our prison. Set us free and close this place.*

She awoke from one such dream, her chemise damp, her hair hanging in thin strands around her face. She rose from her bed and looked out the window into the moonlit night. She considered what the poor invalids must be suffering right now inside the damp, murky cave. She thought of going to the cave herself and seeing what was happening. Instead, she waited until her heart calmed and her breathing returned to normal, recalling the good things that had happened since coming to this place. They were helping people see the glory of Mammoth Cave. If only she could convince Jared that no one here had evil intentions, and the cave certainly wasn't full of evil, either. It was the men Jared associated with who were evil, mad men ignited by their wrath, their swarthy faces filled with rage, the orange flame of the lanterns reflecting in their angry eyes. They were a danger to all she knew and to her family's very existence.

But she also wanted to understand Jared's point of view. His pain and grief. His mission of justice—or so he felt. His concerns rose above evil intentions. He wanted the cave closed only to save people from the agony he now endured. She couldn't help but be intrigued by his plea, even if she disagreed with his intent.

At breakfast, her brothers and father exchanged loud chatter about the previous evening's encounter. Susanna found her appetite gone, and instead, she focused on their every word.

"We need to get a constable here to protect us," Luke insisted, slathering butter on his biscuit. "Someone from Brownsville, maybe. The doctor mentioned he knows men from Louisville. Anyone who can come keep the peace." He swallowed down the bread in two gulps.

Susanna looked at him in disgust. *All this concern doesn't seem to have affected your appetite*, she thought.

"I don't trust any of those varmints that came here last night," Luke continued. "They may come back next time and start shooting."

"One had a gun on him, too!" Henry added. "I saw it."

"Well, I don't want Susanna to be involved in the tours any longer," Mother added. "It's too dangerous for a young lady."

Susanna lifted her head at this comment. "Mother?"

"I wish you to stay inside the hotel. We have seen the ruffians and rogues lurking around. It's too dangerous to have you speaking with the visitors or helping with the tours. For all we know, those men might come back again, maybe even disguised as some visitors, and they might try to harm you. They are of an evil sort."

She recalled Jared's concern for good and not evil. "Mother, Jared said they aren't planning anything evil. They are only concerned about more people being hurt by living in the cave."

"Jared!" Luke announced. "Who's Jared?"

Suddenly all eyes were focused on her. She set down her biscuit and dropped her head. A rush of warmth filled her cheeks.

"Susanna's going courtin'," Henry said in glee.

Her cheeks flushed even deeper. "Henry, shush. I am not. I don't even know the man."

"You know him enough to mention his name and his words," Luke added, picking up another biscuit.

"Maybe you should tell us about this young man, Susanna," Papa said, staring at her. "Was he with the men who came the other evening?"

"Yes. His name is Jared Edwards, and he told me they only wanted to make sure no one else dies inside the cave. And he asked me to help."

"Man alive!" Luke cried, throwing the biscuit on his plate. "Help him do what?"

"Help him close the cave, I think."

"What?" Her parents and brothers shook their heads in dismay. "Why would some varmint be asking you to help close down the cave?" Luke demanded.

Susanna flushed, wondering if she should mention the flowers that she had given for the burial of Jared's aunt and how the gesture had somehow stirred them both. Instead, she shrugged and said, "I don't know."

Luke sat back in his seat with a thud. "Papa, this is worse than we thought. Now they are sending no good varmints like this Jared to set designs on Susanna and use her against us!"

"You aren't to leave this hotel without a chaperone, Susanna," Mother added, her voice rising.

"Mother, really. He means no harm."

"He certainly does!" Luke shouted. "He wants to put us

out of business. And he wants to use you to do his evil work. Don't you care in the least what this man is trying to do?"

Susanna felt frustration rising within her. She came to her feet, throwing her napkin on the table. "None of what you say is true," she said, her voice trembling. "The man just lost his aunt. He wants to see people safe. And you treat him and all the rest of them like common criminals."

"They are criminals if they're trying to close down Dr. Croghan and the cave," Luke returned. "That was no pleasant howdy-do they were offering the other night. Those men were bent on seeing us put down, by violence if necessary."

She felt it again. A jab in the ribs, a poke in the arm, a kick in the shin. Her dear brother, making her life miserable once more. Wasn't working here at the cave supposed to have solved their troubles? Did they really find freedom and life here in this place? For Susanna, she found herself drowning once more in a sea of disappointment and no one seemed to care. Life here was no different than on the farm long ago, except that she had nicer dresses and bonnets and a long dining table covered with a bounty of good food. Her happiness was only on the outside—nothing on the inside, in her heart where the need was greatest. Never did anything appear so real to her as at that moment.

"Aren't you going to say anything?" Luke pressed, interrupting her contemplation. "Either you agree to stand with us, or you're a traitor."

"Luke!" Mother exclaimed, aghast.

She stared at each of her family members, and they returned her stare. Slowly she sat back down and took up her napkin, yet inside her heart festered like an open wound.

"That's better," Papa said with a smile. "There will be no more talk of this. Dr. Croghan has everything in good order.

I will abide by your mother's wishes, Susanna, and have you here helping with the ladies. Henry and Luke can assist Mr. Miller with the guests."

"So now I must stay shut up in the hotel like a prisoner?" Susanna demanded. "What crime have I done? All I did was listen to a grieving soul. Isn't that the Christian thing to do?"

"You're already in league with the likes of this Edwards," Luke snarled. "He's causing you to turn against us. And you of all people, Susanna, sitting there in your fine dress. Where would any of us be unless we had the cave and our work here? Would you rather we be digging up rocks and living in a one-room cabin? Perhaps Mother should find that ratty calico you used to wear to make you see reason rather than listening to the dribble of some hateful farmer who wants to see us all destroyed."

Susanna pressed her lips shut. As much as she wanted to rebuke her brother, nothing she could say or do would change anyone's mind. Her words would only fall on deaf ears, as they seemed to do in recent days. The change had to come from God alone.

After breakfast, Susanna wandered out to the field nearby. There she spent time gathering lilies, the same flowers used in the bouquet she had given to Jared. There was something beautiful about the flowers, with their rich petals arranged to drink deeply of the sun's rays. Pressing a lone flower against her heart, she returned to the hotel and her room where her Bible lay on the table. She pressed the flower between the pages of her Bible near a verse in the Song of Solomon that read, "Set me as a seal upon thine heart, as a seal upon thine arm. . ."

Is this our covenant and our seal, Jared? she wondered. *This flower? Our tying bind that has brought us together, even if we are worlds apart in what we believe to be true?*

❧

It didn't take long for the rooms of the hotel to close in around Susanna. Her heart yearned for the freedom of the woods and even the gust of cold air from the cave's entrance. Seeing the visitors that still came, even with news of the neighboring folk who were angry with Dr. Croghan, made her yearn to help. They were of a curious lot, looking not only for a wonder to behold but to see the place that brought so much attention. Some commented about the night the men appeared. Others asked if the cave would now close. Papa and Mr. Miller vehemently denied that would happen.

None of it mattered to Susanna, who quickly grew bored by her new routine. She wandered about the rooms, her spirit as restless as wildflowers caught in a fierce wind. She felt the petals of her spirit torn asunder by all these goings-on in her life. How dare Luke tell her she was a traitor just because she had given away a bit of her heart to someone in need? Had they all become so callous and unfeeling in this place that they couldn't pity another? Isn't that why Dr Croghan built the cottages inside the cave in the first place? To help? Or had he done it only for his own good fortune and name, forsaking the invalids for selfish gain?

The more Susanna considered this, the more she thought that, perhaps, she should see for herself what was going on inside the cave. Though Mother had forbidden it, Susanna didn't see any reason why she couldn't look inside. Perhaps it might settle things in her mind. She was desperate for peace in a time that had seen nothing but turmoil and confusion.

While Mother was busy doing some embroidery, Susanna slipped out a side door of the hotel. She caught sight of Martha, who lingered by the door and inquired if Susanna needed anything.

"I'm only going out for a bit of air," Susanna told her. "You needn't tell Mother I've left."

Martha opened her mouth to question her, then nodded. "Jes be back soon, Miss Susanna. Don't want no fussin' from yer mammy now. She be real mad."

"Just pretend you never saw me." She nodded curtly and hurried outside.

A small group of people milled about in front of the hotel, Luke among them. The last tour of the day had just finished, and as usual, the visitors were full of exclamations over what they had seen. Drawing in a deep breath to summon her courage, Susanna slipped past the group and down the wide path through the grove of trees, heading for the cave's entrance. From afar, she could hear the trickle of water pouring into the mouth of the cave as if heaven itself were giving the place a drink. A breath of cool dampness brushed her face. The cave's interiors brought forth an eerie feeling. Pausing on a rise just above the opening, she suddenly realized she had no lantern. Without a means of light, she would not be able to venture far before daylight gave way to total darkness.

Sighing, Susanna retraced her steps up the path. Beyond the hotel lay the cemetery. All at once, she caught sight of a shadowy figure hunched over one of the tombstones. Her heart raced. Drawing closer, she could make out the form of a man, his apparel too worn and disheveled for him to be one of the wealthy and refined hotel patrons.

Despite her apprehension, Susanna stepped forward. Leaves crunched beneath her slippers. "Hello?" Her voice echoed through the narrow valley. Susanna paused, startled by the loudness of her own voice, and glanced around to make certain no one from the hotel was in a position to overhear her. Seeing no one on the hotel grounds, she summoned her courage and called out once more to the man in the cemetery. "Hello?"

He never even turned to look her way but kept his vigil at the grave. A chill swept over her. She should leave and return to the hotel where she belonged, but the sadness surrounding the person made her stay.

At last, he turned toward her, but his face and form remained hidden in the evening shadows. "It's me," he said. "Jared Edwards."

Jared! His voice had echoed in her mind since the night they talked. He had come to visit his aunt's grave and, perhaps, to nurse his feelings of depression and disillusionment. He stepped forward wearing homespun pants, muddy from the fields, a rumpled shirt, and suspenders. His hat lay low over his head. From where she stood, she could see the shocks of brown hair poking out from beneath the hat. Beard stubble shadowed his chin. He certainly wasn't anything to look at. No appearance of a gentleman. Nothing of outward value. And his inner spirit emanating only sadness.

"Have you thought about what I said the other night?" he asked. "About helping me close the cave?"

"I am sorry about your aunt, but closing down the cave won't bring her back."

She turned and suddenly felt his hand on her arm, grasping it in a firm hold. Screams clogged her throat. She looked toward the hotel. No one was in sight. *Dear God, help me!*

"I won't hurt you," he said, his voice husky. "I only want to make you understand." Just as quickly, he released her and set his hat back on his head. His walnut-colored eyes gazed at her.

"We've had this conversation already, Mr. Edwards. There is nothing else I can say or do. As it is, I'm already suffering for having spoken to you the other night."

"What do you mean?"

She opened her mouth, ready to spill out her own pain, the rebuke of her family, the scorn of her brother Luke. "It's nothing."

He stood silent for a moment. "What's your name?"

She stepped back, startled by the suddenness of the question. "Susanna. Susanna Barnett."

"Susanna." The name rolled of his tongue. She liked the way his deep voice said it, much to her chagrin. "Susanna, I believe this cave is a danger to you, your family, and everyone else. I wouldn't say it if I didn't believe it. How much more grief must come from this place for you to see what I mean? How many more people have to die? But you do nothing."

She bristled. "I'll have you know, Mr. Edwards, that I have done far more to help you than you could possibly realize." If only he could know.

His face softened to a tender expression at these words, as if he had suddenly found a comrade in battle.

"What I mean is, I understand that you are grieving for your aunt's death," she went on. "I believe that we all should bear one another's burdens in times like this, as scripture says."

He blew out a fine breath. "So you do understand. Only God could have given you a heart of mercy." He stepped forward. "In your heart you must want to help."

"Mr. Edwards, I will not help close down the cave, if that's what you mean."

Her forceful rebuke appeared to stagger him. "But you just spoke about bearing one another's burdens?"

"I said only that I understood your loss. That doesn't mean I agree with what you or your uncle wish to do here. I'm sorry."

A shadow of disappointment crossed his face. "I'm sorry,

too, Miss Barnett. I can tell you are a fine woman, but this cave has taken possession of you like everyone else. It's made you all prisoners."

She gaped at him. "It most certainly has not. . ."

He continued. "It's hard to break free from a place like that. But you have to see with your heart instead of your eyes. 'All things are lawful for me, but I will not be brought under the power of any.' " He turned, gazing at the narrow hollow that led to the cave's entrance. "This place has a power unlike anything I've seen. Even I was taken in by it at first. I thought it was a place for the miraculous and surrendered my aunt to its care. But I've seen the end result. Death to everything I know."

"I'm sorry for that, but life still goes on, Jared. It has to. Jesus even said, 'Let the dead bury their dead.' So you need to stop burying your aunt and start living again."

When she caught his gaze, his eyes looked wild, like some wounded animal. He paused, shook his head, turned, and then took off into the woods. Susanna stood for many moments. Though the words had stung, it only made her wonder more about him. If only she could understand him—and he, her. Could that ever be possible?

six

He shut his eyes against his inner pain. How could a beautiful woman like that be so unfeeling? Where was the graceful doe he'd witnessed that terrible day, the one who gathered the flowers for his aunt's burial, the one who sympathized with his circumstances? How could she say things that hurt worse than the pain he was already feeling? That cave had made her like a blind guide. They were all blind guides leading the blind in that place. They saw nothing but their power and profit amassed at the expense of the weak and helpless. And he thought Susanna, above all the others, would separate herself from the greedy tyranny as she had that day. She had, after all, borne witness to their grief when no one else cared. But it was not to be. The place had taken hold of her as it had everyone else.

"Hi-yup," he ordered the horse, tugging on the reins. The animal obeyed, pulling the plow between the newly planted corn rows that had yet to embrace the sunshine. He hoped to get the plowing out of the way before his uncle appeared. Uncle Dwight had left on some mysterious errand, so Jared took the time to do what he had promised even before Aunt Mattie went to the cave—to care for his uncle's fields. Some would think him helpful and that he was a good Christian. He didn't see it that way. He worked to occupy his thoughts instead of sitting alone in his cabin, consumed by his troubles, wrestling with Susanna's rebuke. Nearly every night he prayed to God to release him from it all, to ease these burdens, or at least make them more bearable. Instead, they hung on him like heavy burdens, pulling him into a pit.

"Whoa," he commanded, pulling back on the reins. He wiped the line of sweat from his brow. Jared tried to make sense out of all this. Were they not sheep in the Lord's pasture? Didn't the sheep hear His voice? As a Christian, wasn't he supposed to hear God's voice? Wasn't it God's voice that told him to send Mattie to the cave? The voice that said there might something special in Susanna? Then why wasn't anything turning out right? Why did Aunt Mattie die? Why did Susanna have to be like the others at that cave, leeches that drained money from the living and now the dead? "Why, God?" he said loudly.

The horse nickered and turned its head as if to inquire of Jared's troubles.

"It's nothing," he told the animal. "Pa and Ma should be about ready to leave St. Louis and go out West, and I'm here with nothing." He leaned against the plow. "Maybe I should go, too. Head for St. Louis. Be a part of that new wagon team. Start new. What is here for me, anyway?" He kicked at a clod of hard soil. "Nothing, that's what."

The horse returned his gaze to the field before him and whinnied.

"I get the message. Keep plowing. Keep going. What does the Good Book say? Keep looking forward? No one's fit for the Lord's kingdom if he keeps looking back?" *Am I still fit for Your kingdom, Lord?* he asked in his heart. *Or is the past keeping me back, away from You and from my future?*

Just then, Jared saw a dust cloud rise in the distance. A rider was coming up the road, fast and furious. Jared wiped the sweat away once more and ambled through the field to the road. The rider bore the dusky face of a man of color. "Whoa, yip," the man called to his horse. "I'm lookin' for a Mistuh Jared Edwards."

"Yes, sir, that's me."

The man straightened, a bit surprised. "Did you just call me suh?"

"Why not? We are all God's men. We're created in His image."

He laughed and tipped back his hat. "Not many folks think of us the way you do. They think we's just some kinda animal or sumthin'."

"That's why I refuse to own anyone. If someone wants to work for me, I'll pay them."

"Woo-wee. Now that's sumthin' I shore would like. How much you figger you'd pay fer me helpin' in that there field?" He pointed to the barren field.

"It's not my field. I'm working it for my uncle. But if I did have a field this big and I had a good money crop, I'd hire you. And we would talk a fair price for the labor."

"Then you remember me when you git yerself that there field. Matt's the name." His dark hand clasped Jared's in a firm handshake. "I work at the cave."

Jared stepped back when heard these words. "You work at the cave? You mean Dr. Croghan's cave?"

"Shore do. Even help guide in the cave. Though Stephen does most of it. He's the big guide there. He knows more about that place than anyone does. Why, he's seen things a person cain't hardly believe."

Despite his opinion of the cave and all the misery it had wrought, Jared couldn't help the curiosity that bubbled up within. "Like what?"

"Oh, let's see. A big rock they call the Giant's Coffin. Ain't nevah seen no giant though. Ha! There's a pit that goes on forever, amen. Ain't no end to it, no suh. Dropped my torch down there once. Just disappeared."

"What?"

"A bottomless pit. Stephen used some wood planks there to cross it when he saw it so's he could get to the other side. He twernt skeered one bit, no suh. Can you imagine falling into a pit like that now? See yer years fly by you, you would."

"I guess so," Jared said slowly, trying to imagine such a sight as a pit that went on forever.

"Oh, and Stephen dun find himself fish without eyes in the river that goes underground there. After a place called Winding Way."

"Fish without eyes? In an underground river?"

"Yep. Guess the good Lawd knows them fish don't need eyes if they live in a cave. What's there to see in all that dark? Cain't see yer hand in front of yer face anyways. I've been there with the lantern snuffed out. Cain't see a thing." He laughed. "Though sometimes I think I can. Just my mind playin' tricks, ya know."

Jared stared in awe and, for the briefest moment, he envisioned the cave, not as a place of danger and destruction but one of wonder and intrigue. He considered what else such a place held until he saw the man take out a folded piece of paper from inside his ratty coat.

"Got a letter here for you."

A letter for me? Who would be writing me? He could scarcely believe it as he took the sealed communication. "Uh. . .thank you."

"Shore thing. Gotta go. Don't you forget me now when you git yerself that land, you hear? Name's Matt." The man flicked the reins and the horse took off.

Jared stared down at the letter with his name clearly written on it. He found himself a stump to sit on and slowly broke the seal. He unfolded the thick brown paper.

Dear Mr. Edwards,

I beg you to excuse my rude behavior at the hotel the other day. I hope you will forgive me. I have considered what you said. I want you to know that I am trying to understand. I do hope you will try to understand my life here, also, so we might come to a reasonable agreement. I believe this is what the Lord would have us do.

Most respectfully, I am,
Susanna Barnett
Mammoth Cave Hotel
Edmonson County, Kentucky

He reread the note three times but still couldn't quite believe it. He gazed upward. Sunlight streamed through the trees with leaf buds just beginning to burst open on the warm wind of a fine spring day. How thankful he was that Susanna had taken the time to write him and share her thoughts. He was glad to see her thinking and considering his side. Beneath the hard woman there was still the glimmer of the one who had held the bouquet of flowers. On the heels of this, too, he realized his own stubbornness. They'd both been argumentative that day, each seeking to convince the other of their own opinions—and both had remained as stony and hard as the cave they debated. They needed more understanding, more of that Christian love and forbearance, a heart of flesh.

He folded the letter and stowed it away in his pocket before ambling back to the horse and plow. "Now what do I do?" he asked. The animal once more turned its head. These must be answers to his prayer, both the talk by the man named Matt and now the letter by Susanna Barnett. Was God slowly unveiling his future? If so, what was it exactly? Surely his future could not include someone like Susanna. Proud Susanna in her fine dresses, store-bought bonnets, slippers that had never touched the mud of a field, the sweet scent of flowers that drifted on the wind whenever she came near. These signs must mean something else.

"Let's go," he told the horse. Soon his uncle would return and there was still a good deal of field left to plow. He wanted to be long gone before Uncle Dwight arrived so as to avoid a confrontation.

He sighed as he drove the plow forward. Uncle Dwight and Susanna. And in between them a bottomless pit, eyeless fish in an underground river, and the darkness that was Mammoth Cave. All parts to some great plan yet to unfold, he was certain.

❧

As twilight began to fall, Jared saw another cloud of dust and heard the rattling of a wagon. He hastened to drive the horse and plow back into his uncle's barn just as Uncle Dwight appeared over the horizon, accompanied by several men on horseback. Many of the men Jared recognized from the confrontation at the hotel, including George Higgins and others. Not all the men held a grievance with Dr. Croghan and the cave. Some were simply angry for anger's sake and wanted a quarrel to give them something to do. Each man dismounted, wearing a hardened face and rugged clothing, stained with the sweat of labor in the fields. Some carried guns. One held stubbornly to his jug of liquor.

Jared stepped back into the barn, wondering why they came armed. Were they thinking of returning to the hotel again tonight? All at once, he envisioned Susanna, clad in her snow-white dress, her eyes wide with terror, pleading for help from the ruffians that had come to terrorize them. Despite his apprehension, Jared hurried out of the barn to find out what was afoot.

Uncle Dwight whirled and aimed his gun. "Who's there?"

"Just me, Uncle."

"Howdy, Jared," Higgins said good-naturedly.

"Git off my land!" Dwight shouted. "You got no right here."

"Don't be so hard on him, Dwight," Higgins said. "Jared's a good fellar."

"Good for what, I'd like to know," Dwight muttered, leading the way into the cabin, followed by the men who all talked at once.

Jared threw aside his fear and entered the cabin on their heels. Despite what his uncle said, he was linked to the cave as much as they were and maybe more so. He would be a part of this whether they wanted him there or not.

"So what do you think?" asked a man named Abe Nichols, who poured out his potent brew into cups for all. When he offered the liquor to Jared, Jared shook his head. The odor made him sick to his stomach.

"We have no choice," Dwight said. "They ain't gonna budge, even if you think they are, Higgins."

"I'd just as soon give them more time before we do something we might regret," Higgins claimed. "We only talked to that doctor once. We need to keep after him."

"Once is enough in my opinion," Dwight declared. "Time to show him and all the rest of them highfalutin folk that we mean what we say."

Jared stared from one man to the other, even as a dread

filled him. *Lord, what are they planning?*

"Hey, and what happened with that girl you know?" Higgins asked Jared. "You talk to her? She gonna help?"

All eyes focused on Jared. He looked at each face tense with determination, anger, bitterness, revenge. "I don't think she can do anything."

Dwight slapped the table. "There, you see? They ain't gonna do nuthin', I tell you. We're just wasting time. I say we blow 'em to kingdom come."

Jared stared. Again, he suppressed his fear and asked with as calm a voice as he could muster, "So, how do you all plan to deal with this problem?"

"We got ourselves a good plan," said Abe, combing his beard with his fingers. "I got me some good powder."

"We're gonna blow up that no-good cave," Dwight snarled. "Seal it up good so no one can go in there ever again and no highfalutin doctor can make money on the misery of others."

Blow up the cave? He looked to Higgins. Surely he couldn't agree with such a plan. "What do you say about this, Mr. Higgins?"

Higgins took a swig of the brew in his tin cup before wiping his hand across his mouth. "Well, I still think we ought to try and do some more talking."

"Not only that, but you could end up killing innocent people!" Jared added.

Their eyes once again focused on him.

"Ha!" Dwight cried, standing to his feet, his breathing ragged. "And you talk about us killin', after my Mattie died on account of you."

"Now, Dwight," Higgins began. "You can't blame Jared for that. He was trying to help. He had no idea she was gonna die. None of us knew we'd lose our loved ones in that place."

His uncle settled back in his chair, muttering. Jared gave Higgins what he hoped was a look of gratitude.

"And we ain't gonna kill no one," said Abe. "At least I ain't. I just wanna make sure the cave is sealed up. I'm tired of all the fussing about it and the fancy folk coming here by stage to see it. Not a moment's peace around here."

"But people still live in the cave," Jared protested, ignoring the look of anger painted on Uncle Dwight's face. "You seal it shut, and they could be trapped. How can you bury people alive?"

The men grew quiet then, mulling over his words. Even Dwight stayed silent.

"Jared is right," Higgins declared. "I think we need to let the talking do the work. We'll meet again with the doctor. Lean on him harder than we have been. I think we did rattle them by showing up like we did the other night. So we'll keep it up, and I believe we're gonna see a change."

Jared exhaled slowly, thankful for Higgins's support that put the scheme of violence to rest—at least for the time being. He touched Susanna's letter in his pocket. He couldn't bear to see terror grip her should some explosion rock her home. There had to be other ways to resolve these differences.

"You got some wisdom in you," Higgins commented to Jared when the meeting concluded. He strode over to his mount and patted the animal before gathering up the reins. "Ought to git my ornery son to listen to you instead of him taking off into the hills like he does. He could learn a heap."

"You don't think anyone's gonna blow up the cave, do you, Mr. Higgins?"

"Not now," he said with a grunt, hoisting himself into the saddle and bringing the animal about. "But it's really up to Dr. Croghan what happens next. And I must say, if he wants to avoid trouble, he'd better come up with a solution to this."

"And what if he doesn't?"

"Don't know, Jared. You heard what was said. Look, I had someone close to me die in that cave. Don't you think that place should be closed up? It buried our kin. It should be buried, too. No one should be able to visit there anymore. It's like holy ground, I guess you could say."

"I don't know, sir. I didn't look at it that way."

"Well, maybe you should. Then maybe you would see why your uncle and the others think the way they do." With a *yah* he galloped off down the road.

A wave of dread came over Jared as he leaned over the fencing. *God, what is happening with everyone?* Here he'd thought Higgins might feel as he did, avoiding violence at all cost and seeking whatever peace could be found in the situation. But if things did not go as planned, Higgins could not be trusted either. *God, please don't let it come to violence*, he prayed.

seven

Jared must have read Susanna's letter at least a dozen times over the course of the past few days. Meanwhile, the fields lay untended, the eggs still in the chicken coop, and the wood unsplit as he sat on the porch step of his humble cabin and stared at the sheet of paper. Even thoughts of the meeting with his uncle and friends rapidly faded away. Instead, he imagined her forming the words with each stroke of the instrument dipped in ink, her blue eyes focused on the sentences she wrote, spelling out her heart. At least, he thought her eyes were blue. He wasn't certain. He hadn't really gotten a good look at her eyes, what with the encounter in the cemetery coming as dusk fell. At least he knew her hair was the color of brown sugar. And she wore fine dresses. The mark of a true lady, rich and proud.

He looked around at his cabin. He once thought this place to be the best thing he had ever built. Now thinking of Susanna, it looked small and shabby, unfit for a woman of her means. He wiped his hand across his eyes. Why would he be thinking of Susanna living here of all places? She was used to a castle, the hotel with its fine furniture and fancy folk. He was but a humble farmer. She would never consent to a life like this—and with him of all men.

Yes, his uncle had made good money growing cash crops, and he had taken his fair share of the profits. He had money to his name. But his family always did live simply. He never once considered deserting this humble cabin for a house of brick or stone, with fine furniture on which to rest easy. As his aunt always said, it was good to have extra money on hand for special needs and not to spend it on foolish pleasantries. One didn't know if the plow might break, a horse would need shod, or someone would happen by who could use a helping hand.

Jared stood to his feet and entered his little cabin to look at the money accrued in the jar. There was plenty to spare—money even to buy Susanna something special. Maybe enough to buy her heart and abandon the hotel life to take up residence with him. That would be grand. But is that what he wanted to do? Buy her understanding and her love?

He pushed away the thought and stuffed some of the money into his pocket. He needed provisions from town anyway. Salt pork. Beans. Tea. Maybe he'd get his uncle some of that horehound candy he fancied. And maybe Susanna might enjoy a few sweets as well. A small token, really. He could sweeten up both her and Uncle Dwight at the same time. Make them see that he wasn't an awful person, that he was someone they both could trust.

Jared saddled one of the two horses he owned, the fine tan mare his father had left him. A journey to Brownsville would be a nice diversion from the myriad of thoughts that swirled in his head these days. Soon he was on his way, deciding to make the most of this pleasant spring day. The air felt warm and soothing on his face. The grass had begun to green up, and a few more flowers began their showy display of color, like the violets and pink columbine. It all reminded him of the work he still needed to do. He should be home planting the fields and not heading to town. But other things drove his heart and spirit at the moment, like a lovely young woman who had taken the time to write him when he needed it most.

He wasn't good with words or he would write back. In his eyes, a gift would say it all.

Presently he saw a stately coach heading toward him on the rough road with horses prancing. The driver lifted his hand to Jared, signaling him to stop. The door of the coach opened, and a gentleman peered out.

"Good morning. I'm Otis Clark. Whom do I have the pleasure of addressing?"

Jared steadied his mount with a firm grip on the reins. "Jared Edwards. What can I do for you?"

"We would like to know where the cave is. Mammoth Cave, that is. Can you direct us?"

He felt the heat crawl into his cheeks at the mere mention of the place. It conjured up memories both good and bad—bad on account of his aunt's passing, good by way of Susanna.

"The one owned by a certain doctor," the man continued. "Surely you've heard of it. We came all the way from Philadelphia just to see it."

Jared pondered this. Should he tell them to have a good trip and direct them to the right road? Or should he tell them the cave was dangerous? That it hurt people, and they would do better to return home? If he didn't warn them, wouldn't he be a hypocrite?

He cleared his throat. "Yes, I know of it. But I must warn you, there are strange diseases afoot in that place."

"What?" A woman's face now appeared beside Otis Clark's, the bow of her bonnet tickling the man's face. "Did I hear there is some disease in the cave?"

Jared removed his hat. "Yes, ma'am, a bad disease there. Several have died. Including my own aunt."

"We've only heard from friends what an interesting place

the cave is," claimed the gentleman. "There are tours and everything."

"They have tours. But with the disease and all, it's just too dangerous to go there."

The man and woman looked at each other. "And we came all this way," she pouted. "How can this be?"

"Don't fret, my dear. It must be providential that this young man is warning us of the danger." He glanced back once more at Jared. "What disease is it, may I ask?"

"Consumption."

The woman's hand flew to her mouth in aghast. "Oh no! How dreadful! Otis, please tell the driver to take us away from here. I don't want to be anywhere near that cave. Think of our children!" She went on, even as she settled back in her seat. "This is terrible. How can they be conducting tours there when there are people dying inside?"

"Thank you," Otis called out before ordering the driver to turn around.

Jared sat still on his mount, watching the coach slowly turn and proceed back down the road from whence it came. Suddenly his desire to go to Brownsville to buy Susanna a gift had likewise been rerouted. He had just sent back people who would have come to tour the cave and feed money into the purses of Susanna's family and, yes, Susanna herself. Nevertheless, he had no choice. Some things were more important than money—like people's lives. Susanna had to realize it. They all did.

Jared looked down the long road that led to Brownsville and decided to continue. If nothing else, he would still lay in provisions at the store. And maybe a small bit of candy for his uncle to sweeten his sour spirit. But anything for Susanna would have to wait for a long time, he feared. Especially if she discovered how he had chased patrons away from her cave.

❧

Brownsville, nestled beside the Green River, was the only thriving community in these parts. The small, close-knit town served the needs of travelers and farmers alike. There was the general store, a mill, an iron forge, and a hotel boasting fine mineral springs with healing in them, or so the townspeople said. Jared stopped at the general store and anchored his reins to a rail. He hadn't been to town in quite a while. In fact, it may have been before his aunt died. He recalled coming here with Uncle Dwight, seeing friends, talking about the crops. The friends had inquired about Aunt Mattie's health, with a sideways glance toward Jared. Dwight said he expected her to do just dandy in the cave, and when spring came, to be as healthy as any of them.

Jared swallowed hard at the thought. Now he came here alone, without his aunt or his uncle. The realization convinced him that he had made the right decision to warn the rich folk about avoiding Mammoth Cave. He would do it again if he must. Perhaps he might even put up announcements around Brownsville and at Bell's Tavern, warning travelers not to go there. Maybe that would force the doctor to close. Even if it made Susanna and others angry, he believed it was the right thing to do.

He took off his hat and climbed the set of stairs to the store, stopping short at the window. A young woman stood at the counter, chatting away with the clerk. He wiped his eyes. She had many fine objects spread out before her. He came to the window for a closer look. A new hat lay on the counter. A brush and comb. Some hairpins. A book. All very expensive items.

Just then, the woman turned and pointed at the cracker barrel. When he saw her face, Jared sucked in his breath. *Susanna Barnett!* He looked once more at the fineries. It was not the sight of the pretty woman that stirred his heart. He only saw frivolous objects—fineries purchased in exchange for the lives of his aunt and others inside a cave. He whirled away, sickened by the sight. How could she do such a thing? Exactly what was she trying to make him understand in that letter of hers? That she needed the cave's money to buy her fancy things? That she cared nothing about where the money came from? That she cared nothing for the misery of others?

"Yes, and thank you, Mr. Hensley," Susanna called back as a young boy helped her carry the items she had purchased to an awaiting wagon.

Jared wanted to turn away and never look back, but he couldn't. He could not let this pass. He stood his ground on the porch, his hat low on his head, as the errand boy walked past carrying the goods. Susanna came out of the store next, her face relaxed, a small smile sitting on her lips, her dress sweeping the wooden flooring of the porch.

He took a step forward. "Susanna."

She stepped back in response. "Oh!"

"It's me. Jared Edwards."

"Mr. Edwards! You startled me. Isn't this a surprise? Are you here to visit the general store?"

"In a matter of speaking."

"A fine spring day to shop, isn't it?"

"I suppose fine for a few things." He tipped his hat back. "Like buying heaps of fine goods."

She drew her tiny brocade handbag farther up her arm. "I don't understand what you mean."

"A fine day for spending cave money on a new bonnet.

Combs. Ribbons. All the necessities of life."

Her face contorted into a mixture of dismay. "I see. Well, pardon me. I must be going. Good day." She brushed by him.

"And, in that letter you sent to me, you talk of understanding?" he pressed, following her. "Is this what I'm supposed to understand? That you have need for all these fripperies? That I might take these niceties away from you if the cave is closed?"

She whirled. "Really, Mr. Edwards. I don't think it's any of your affair what I do with the money God has given me."

"The money God has given you! You talk about God giving you this? God is a God of mercy, not of wanton pleasure."

"A merciful God understands my plight more than you will ever know. And that's because you don't have any of His mercy in you." She headed for the wagon where the driver stood waiting.

"What plight could you have possibly endured in your life?" he went on.

"You don't understand, Mr. Edwards. And you never will, because you are blinded by the very things you want to do away with."

"You're right, I don't. I don't understand how you can take cave money like this and use it for your own selfishness."

Her face reddened. "Nor do I understand how you can judge me without knowing me. And that is what you are doing. Judge not, lest ye be judged." She mounted the wagon with the help of the driver.

"Now you jes go on outta here," the driver told him. "Go on and leave Miss Barnett alone."

Jared bristled. He couldn't let this go, not while he still had breath. "So please tell me, Miss Barnett. What is this plight of yours that I'm supposed to understand?"

"I would tell you if I thought you would pay me any mind at all. But all you see is your own anger. You're no different from your uncle except you're unarmed."

He thought about it, calming himself enough to take a step back and relax his stance. He did want to know everything about her. She intrigued him, much as he hated to admit it. He had nursed her letter as if it was the dearest thing he had ever received. And she really was a beautiful sight to see. "I'll listen. Come with me to the tavern down the road and tell me everything. I will even buy you a cup of tea."

"No, thank you. To the tea, that is." She paused. "But since you asked, I will tell you. You need to know just who and what you are judging." Slowly she eased herself to the ground, sweeping her dress around the wheel. "Wait for me, Solomon. I won't be long."

"Miss Barnett. . . ," Solomon began in protest.

Jared could hardly believe she had agreed to talk to him. Whatever she wanted to say must burn fierce within her, some knowledge he needed to know. Despite his dismay at her fineries, he couldn't help but be taken in by her dress and bonnet. He would take in all of her, her beauty, her dreams, everything about her, if other things weren't clouding his vision at the moment. Maybe it would all be put to rest this day if he but listened.

❧

They walked for a time, away from the bustle of the town and curious onlookers. Soon they were heading into a field, enjoying the feel of the sun on their faces and the breezes that carried the scents of springtime. Jared was amazed at the confidence Susanna had to go with him. She showed no fear but determination. Maybe a matter of trust had already begun to form between them, even if it seemed unbelievable.

Were they not opposing forces, ready to do battle to keep their own purposes alive? Or were they trying to come to an understanding, as she said, and this was the beginning of something new in their lives?

"This looks like a fine place to talk," she said when they came upon a small stream. She found a rock to sit upon, where she spread her dress in a perfect fan across the stony surface. "I love to sit and look at a stream. There's something about water that is so soothing. The Green River flows by Mammoth Cave, too. Some of the visitors come by boat to see the cave."

His anger began to rise. She must know how talking about the cave would infuriate him. Yet she spoke about it as if it were a pleasant conversation to be had on a warm, sunny day.

She continued. "When I was little I would sit on a rock and wonder what my life would be like in the future. What plans God might have for me. And I would look down at my dirty calico dress and wonder if that future might mean I could have a pretty dress to wear one day. And food to eat."

He said nothing, though he had to admit his curiosity had been piqued by her choice of words.

"I thought about it a lot when we lived in the little cabin I shared with Papa, Mother, and my two brothers. My room in that cabin was the loft. Drafty in winter, hot in summer. I'm sure you know what I mean, Mr. Edwards."

The truth be known, he had never slept in a loft. He had his own room inside his uncle's large cabin. And, of course, once he built his own place, he slept in a small room adjacent to the main cabin. Now he pondered her words. She had slept in a cabin? When? Wasn't that fancy hotel her home?

"Sometimes I would get so cold in winter, I would shiver and come down to warm myself by the fire. Other times I felt like I would die in the heat. Kentucky summers can be hot, as you know. Once I even took off in the middle of the night to take a dunking in the stream. Mother was angry when she found out. But I didn't care. And it felt wonderful, that cool water on a hot summer's night."

Jared plucked a reed and began to chew on it. Where did she get these stories? From some visitor? Maybe one of the servants working at the cave? Surely it couldn't be a tale of her life.

"And when it would come time for the meals, I would go out to the garden and dig up a potato or two. Papa tried to get a plow through the ground. He had bought the land with all the money he had. But he didn't know until later that he was sold a land full of rocks. It grew nothing for him. What potatoes and other vegetables we grew became our food. Potato soup. Some corn for cornbread. Hardly any money to buy chickens or any of the salt pork at the store. Just potato soup and cornbread. Day after day. Mother made it last as long as she could."

He stopped gnawing on the reed to let the description sink in. He wanted to say something but found his mind blank.

"And then came the accident on the road. I was talking to God by a stream like this one. Luke had just upset my soup over the only dress I had, a ripped calico. I came to the stream to pray when I heard a terrible noise." She glanced up then, her blue eyes luminescent as they reflected the sunlight. "A wagon had overturned, and a man was pinned underneath. It was Dr. Croghan. I ran for Papa and my brothers. We helped him to our cabin, and he stayed for few days. Afterwards, as a thank you, he asked us to come work for him at his hotel. We left the cabin and never looked back." She paused to throw a small stone into the stream. "From then on, I cast all my cares away. I never want to look back. No matter what." She turned to eye him. "I know you think I'm selfish and that I don't care. But I do care. I know what it's like to have nothing at all. And since God has blessed me with a few things of worth, then I will take His blessing and be thankful."

Jared could offer no words in reply. Either she had just told him the most emotional lie to convince him of her opinions, or she had witnessed the trials of life that nearly drove her family to the brink of despair, if not for the intervention of Dr. Croghan.

"You aren't saying anything," she noted, taking off her bonnet. The breezes blew the curly, brown-sugar ringlets that framed her face. "You don't believe me, do you? You think I made this up. You think I'm a spoiled, pampered, rich girl who knows nothing of hardship. But it isn't true. None of it. I've lived it all."

"I believe you."

His reply must have caught her by surprise. She had opened her mouth, poised to offer a further rebuke, but instead smiled. "Then I would say we are definitely on the road to some manner of understanding, Mr. Edwards."

"Jared," he corrected, staring intently at her upturned lips. "Call me Jared. Mr. Edwards is my father."

"And where is your father? Your family? I haven't seen them, have I?"

"I don't know where they are."

Her forehead crinkled in puzzlement "What do you mean? What happened to them?"

He relished the concern in her voice that proved comforting. A genuine concern. Not made up. Not pretend. Just like the day his aunt died. She was a woman who cared. He was convinced of it now, more than ever. "I don't really know.

They wanted to go out West. They left here when they heard of wagon trains soon to make their way to Oregon Territory. They left last year, headed for St. Louis. I haven't heard from them since. For all I know, they may have already left."

"But why didn't you leave with them? Why did you stay here in Kentucky?"

"I stayed because I was born here. And I met the Lord here through a traveling preacher who came to Kentucky. Besides, I couldn't leave my aunt and uncle alone. Aunt Mattie got sick. Uncle Dwight needed help with the fields. And now look at what's happened." He heard Susanna inhale a swift breath as he broached the topic that separated them from the beginning.

"It must be hard," she said softly. "I can't imagine losing someone so close to me and then not having family around for comfort. Sometimes I wish I didn't have my brothers, as they tend to be quite bothersome. But never would I want to be separated from any of them for very long."

He began to stir with an understanding that gave way to hope—hope that maybe God had begun to open Susanna's eyes. Hope that she was ready to come to Jared's side, even closer than before.

"But I know, too, that God has blessed us and many others with this cave," she went on. "I don't believe the cave is a curse. I believe it's a blessing."

"It can't be both. To you a blessing, to me a curse. We can't both be right, and we can't both be wrong."

They sat in silence together, listening to the water play a melody over the rocks. "Then we must come to a truce," Susanna declared, offering him her hand.

"A truce?" He took her hand in his.

"That while we may disagree, we can still respect and

understand each other with God's help."

And maybe even more, he thought silently. He gazed at her hand, tiny and velvety white against his rough skin. He never felt anything so soft. He held onto it, savoring the feel of it. He caressed the top of her hand with his thumb.

Her cheeks pinked. Her hand shifted in his. "Jared?" she asked softly.

The feel of her hand. The look of her face. Eyes blue like the feathers of a bluebird. Parted lips so inviting. Dare he even think of kissing her? Dare he consider her in such a fashion, as one he could come to know, to love, and even to marry? He dropped her hand and stared off into the distance. At least he did have some understanding now—an understanding that birthed something new in him. He prayed she might consider him in a new light, as well, even beneath the image of a Kentucky farmer in dusty boots.

"Maybe we can meet again?" he wondered, somewhat shyly.

"I'd like that very much."

He sighed. Hope was alive and well. He left Brownsville with an excitement in his heart, ready to face whatever came next.

eight

She whispered his name in the night shadows when the moon rose full in the sky and bathed the Kentucky landscape in a veil of white. She looked often at her hand, the one he held in his, and remembered the way his gaze never left hers. It was as if he searched her heart to see what lay inside, much like those who searched the cave for priceless treasure. Something had drawn them together, even if they were still far apart. They lived in two separate worlds, each with its own manner of thinking. She would not relinquish the cave of prosperity, and he would never let go of his claim that the cave meant death. They seemed at an impasse, yet they had come to some manner of agreement.

When had the sun risen in the sky, along with the moon?

"Hello! Is your mind far across the ocean again?" Luke had come up, carrying caving costumes for the visitors. "We are here to conduct business, Susanna, or have you forgotten?"

She took the clothing with a halfhearted gesture. "Do you ever think there is more to life than making money?"

Luke glanced up from his work of examining the lanterns to see if they required lard oil. His eyes narrowed to tiny slits. "What kind of a question is that? Have you been talking to that man Jared again?"

She put the costumes on a chair and smoothed out her dress. "I don't think that is any of your affair."

"Man alive, you have been talking to him! Susanna, how could you? Are you still willing to betray your own family?"

"I am doing nothing of the sort. If anything, you should be happy that I've been talking to him." She lifted her head high in the air.

"How would you expect me to come to that conclusion?"

"Because Jared knows the men who came here. If I can convince him of the cave's value, I believe he will protect us from them."

Luke snorted. "If you think that, then you are quite naïve. The man has been trying to win you over by his words. He's using you as a spy for his plans. How can you fall for such deception?"

Susanna stared, unable to believe such an insinuation. "He isn't a spy. . . ," she began, even as doubt crept forth. *He couldn't be. He never asked me questions. He never gave such an appearance.*

Luke picked up the lanterns. "A man is wise in his own opinions until corrected by another. You've seen the wisdom in what we are doing here. You wear it proudly every day. Now you could destroy everything we have earned by talking to that man. I'll have to go to Papa about it."

She felt the heat enter her face. "I've done nothing wrong."

He said no more. She watched him leave, the trepidation building. She could envision the look of anger on Papa's face when he heard the news that she had been conspiring with some so-named enemy, planting seeds of destruction in their work. Causing the good doctor and her family to go to ruin. She might be cast away, perhaps to live with poor relatives in Ohio. Papa would order her to leave everything behind, clothed only in sackcloth as penance.

"I've done nothing wrong," she said again, gathering up the cloaks. *If anything, I'm trying to keep terrible things from happening. Jared and I have already begun to come to an understanding. He knows how I feel. And I'm beginning to learn more about him, too, though I wish I knew more.*

She tried to smile at the visitors while handing out the cloaks to protect their fine garments during the tour, but the expression felt forced. There was no joy in this work. There were only questions, wondering what would become of them all. And now, with Luke looking to expose everything that lay hidden in her heart, she became even more distraught.

For now, she tried to cast it all aside. Jared had asked to meet her again for a short walk by the Green River that afternoon. When the tour left, Susanna primped and went in haste to find him waiting in the reeds. The smile he gave warmed her heart. No, Jared may not be a gentleman clad in fine frocks, but he was a gentleman, nevertheless. They strolled along the riverbank, watching bugs skitter across the river's surface. He picked up her hand as he did once before. She liked his touch. He asked about her dreams for the future.

"I don't really know," she confessed. "I can only take tomorrow as it comes. It's enough for me right now." She dare not tell him her dream of the man on the black horse, or of being swept away to a grand home on a hillside, or anything else. She only wanted to live for this moment.

"I've had people tell me I need to think about the future. About things like. . ." He paused. "I guess I'm living one day at a time, too, and letting tomorrow take care of itself." She felt he wanted to say more, but it stayed buried. Instead, she rejoiced in the brief time they had before one of the servants came running to find her. When Jared bid her farewell, appearing saddened that the time had been so short-lived, she only hoped they would meet again soon.

At dinner that night, the family offered her looks of disapproval all around. Susanna panicked, wondering if they somehow knew of her secret walk with Jared earlier that day. They gazed at her as if she had betrayed them. She never felt so alone. How could she tell them that she held no evil intent in speaking with Jared, that she only wanted peace to come from this situation? That Jared was a kind man through and through who only wanted what was best for everyone?

After dinner, Papa called her into the study. He sat down in his chair and waited expectantly. Not long after, the doors opened, and Dr. Croghan himself ventured in, stiff and stern in his frock coat with gleaming brass buttons and polished boots. Susanna felt weak under the gaze of the man who owned the very place where her family lived and worked. Archibald Miller arrived next, equally dressed in fashionable attire, accompanied by a stern expression to match the prevailing atmosphere. She felt even weaker.

They took seats near Papa. "Miss Barnett," they each greeted.

"Dr. Croghan," she managed to say. "Mr. Miller."

The men nodded to her father. "I have something to read to you, Susanna," Papa said, withdrawing a letter.

Susanna sucked in her breath. "Who is it from, Papa?" she asked in as controlled a voice as possible. Could it be from Jared? Did he expound on the love she felt certain was there, like that day in the woods when he held her hand and even during the walk this very afternoon? The idea made her shudder, especially if such a letter had found its way into her father's hands.

He unfolded the letter and cleared his throat. " 'We were most disturbed to find all manner of disease being entertained in your cave. We had traveled far from Philadelphia, intent on seeing this wondrous sight about which we had heard told. Bless providence, we were stopped by a farmer named Jared Edwards who told us of the deaths attributed to the cave.

We now ask that you warn others and put forth the necessary actions to prevent a terrible calamity from happening.' " Pa folded the letter. All the men stared at her grimly. "We know the man who spoke to these people is the same young man you have been meeting in confidence, Susanna."

Jared? But how. . . ? She straightened. "Yes, Papa, I. . .I have seen him a few times."

"And you saw him the night those men came, did you not?" Dr. Croghan asked. "Some say he even seemed to know you."

"He was very disturbed, of course, over his aunt's passing. I saw him for the first time the day she passed away." She wanted to tell him about the grief she witnessed, the flowers she gave, the wrenching of her heart at the harsh words his uncle had spoken. Then the good things that came from it, the day they sat together by the stream when he held her hand and gazed steadfastly into her eyes. The walk by the river this very afternoon when she sensed a knitting together of minds and hearts.

Croghan and Papa exchanged glances. "Hiram, I've been told this is the same Edwards that has been having secret meetings inside his cabin," the doctor said, his frustration evident. "I'm told he's raising a following. And now he's spreading lies among the very populace with which we do business." He turned to acknowledge Susanna who shrank in her seat under his baneful stare. "What do you know about this young man?"

"I—I know he was upset about the cave. He has called it a death cave in the past. I've tried to convince him otherwise, that the cave has many fine features. But I know he isn't raising a following to do us harm. His uncle is very—"

"You see?" Croghan interrupted. "A death cave! This young man has been conspiring in all manner of deceit concerning my cave. And your own daughter is involved, Hiram!"

"Doctor, please." She began feeling more nervous under his glaring countenance. "We have talked, yes. But don't you agree that in pleasant conversation and sympathizing with others we can all come to an understanding?"

"An understanding of what?"

"I. . .uh. . ." She paused, suddenly confused.

"An understanding that my cave is dangerous? That it is now called the Death Cave instead of Mammoth Cave? That it is neither fit for man nor beast and should be closed?" Croghan stood to his feet and began to pace. "No. This can't be allowed to continue. We must put a stop to this. If we don't, I'll have no choice but to close if a ruckus ensues."

"You can't close the cave," Miller protested. "Look at all we've accomplished here."

Susanna saw her father turn pasty white "There must be some other way to resolve this," he said slowly.

"Perhaps a meeting," Miller suggested, "between all of us."

"I will be forced to close unless this situation is resolved," Croghan said grimly. "Already some are urging me to do so after what's happened with the invalids." He whirled to face Susanna. "Since you know this young man, perhaps it would do us well to have both him and his uncle for dinner. Explain the nature of the cave and what we wish to accomplish here. Offer what we can in the manner of sorrow and understanding, as you have said. But at the same time, avoid other difficulties with regards to the cave and its visitors. Do you think your young man will agree to such an invitation?"

"I—I don't know, sir. I'm sure he will wonder what it is about. He will be suspicious. Even when I was making purchases at Brownsville, he. . ." She halted then, realizing what she had said. She didn't want them to know of that day and the encounter by the stream, how something special had been forged between them. "That is, he was most distressed at the idea of making money from a place where his aunt died so tragically."

"You see?" Croghan complained. "No one believes in what we are doing here. Now we have a disease worse than the consumption spreading throughout Kentucky—the disease of spoken lies. And it will be our undoing unless something is done."

"Then it's settled," Miller decided. "We will have the men here for dinner in the hotel's private dining room. We will make it a lavish affair. And pray that good intentions will resolve this situation." Miller pointed to Susanna. "And she must be the one to invite them since she and the young man know each other."

Papa nodded. "Yes, you will personally deliver the invitation, Susanna, since you and the young man seem to have come to some understanding. And I pray this will be resolved. We must keep the tours going at all cost."

Susanna stared at her father. She had hoped he wanted the meeting to restore peace and forge sympathy for the grief caused by the cave. Only by this could they keep Jared and others from warning visitors not to come here. Instead, she saw her father desperate to save his livelihood by any means available. No matter what they said, Jared wouldn't believe it, nor would his uncle. They had been through too much. They would look beyond all this to see the real intent, to keep the cave open despite what they had been through.

"God, help me know what to do in all this," she prayed that night. Now, given the quest of delivering the invitation to Jared and his uncle, she couldn't help her anxiety. Jared and she had both begun to build trust between them. Would this now shatter it all?

❧

On the appointed day of the invitation's delivery, Susanna took extra care in dressing and calmed herself with prayer. Since Matt Bransford knew where Jared lived, having delivered the letter she once wrote to him, she asked Matt to take her there. The pleasant spring day and the birds serenading their ride calmed the nervous fluttering of Susanna's heart. The birds flew from limb to limb along the road, soaring above the difficulties of this life. If God could understand the birds' needs, as scripture said, He must also understand what was about to unfold.

The dampness of her hand made the paper she carried limp. Matt tried to entertain her with stories, but her mind remained consumed by her errand. What would she say when she arrived? How would she confront Jared about the contents of the letter? What would he say in response to it and the invitation? And how would she confront him about what she had learned concerning his conversation with the patrons of the cave?

"Yer awfully quiet, Miss Barnett," Matt observed.

"I'm not sure what to say when I see him," she confessed.

"You mean when you see that young fellar? Why there ain't no reason to fret. He's a fine fellar. We had ourselves a right good talk. He even said I might work the land one day and git paid for it, iffen I can git away from the cave for a spell. Though I don't think Massah Crawn's gonna let me do that."

Susanna glanced over at the man who stared at the road ahead, urging the horses forward. "You talked to Jared?"

"Yes'm, when I delivered that note from you. Pleased he was to git it, I must say. And he dun called me suh, too.

Never had anyone call me suh before. Made me feel right important." He straightened then. "Yes'm, he shore made me feel like I was sumthin'. Don't get that much around here. But he said that the good Lawd made us all. And there ain't no difference in the Lawd's eyes."

Susanna marveled at this. Perhaps there wasn't anything to fear. Jared must possess a bit of a merciful heart to give dignity and honor where honor was due. Maybe all would go well.

"Yes'm, he made my day. I've talked to many a folk in the cave there, but none treat me like that man did. They think I'm just a part of that place, you know. But he knows I got feelings. Yes'm, maybe we can get some things changed around here. We could sure use it."

She liked hearing these descriptions that painted a more appealing picture of Jared than what she had heard of late. She always wanted to know more about him, and it seemed the Lord was opening new doors each day.

The rolling hills surrounding the cave soon gave way to patches of green farmland, where those who tried to make a living off the land had built their homes. She began feeling tense once more as the horses plodded ever nearer to their destination. Matt drove the wagon around a bend in the road and toward a plowed field. "This is the field here where I dun seen the fellar. He ain't there now, though."

Susanna strained to see. "No one is working the fields. Head on up the road a bit."

Matt did so, only to come to a junction in the road. He brought the horses to a standstill. "Well now, I ain't sure where to go, Miss Barnett. This here's the field all right. Maybe he lives close by."

"We'll ask at the next cabin we come to. Keep going

straight." She tucked the lap robe more firmly around herself to protect her dress from the dust and retied the bonnet beneath her chin. There was no turning back. Papa, Mr. Miller, Dr. Croghan, everyone was looking to her to accomplish the task. They wanted her to help them keep the cave open. Jared wanted to see it closed. Why did everyone think she could help?

A simple cabin soon appeared in the distance, not unlike the one in which Susanna had grown up. She caught her breath as memories washed over her from several years ago. She would stop here and inquire.

In the yard, a man was splitting wood with an ax. His hat sat low on his head even as Matt drew the wagon to a stop. He looked up for a moment before swiping off his hat. "Susanna?"

Jared! She nearly leapt from the wagon in relief. God had guided their steps to the very place.

"This is a surprise," Jared said, offering his hand to help her down from the wagon.

From what she could tell, he did look surprised and even pleased. She rearranged her skirts, shaking out the many petticoats.

"What are you doing here?" He glanced at Matt sitting in the wagon before ramming the ax into a stump. "I take it this isn't a social call." He went over to a water barrel to refresh himself, offering her the dipper.

"No, thank you. And, of course, this is a social call. Or rather a social call to bring you an invitation." She wasted no time handing him the letter crafted by Mr. Miller. She watched his dark eyes travel over the words, wondering what he was thinking. He then tucked the note into his pocket and picked up the ax. Confusion and curiosity filled her, watching him lift the ax and bring it to bear on a chunk of wood. "Have you nothing to say?"

"I have plenty to say, but since my uncle is also invited, I can't say one way or the other. So I won't keep you. I'm sure there are things waiting for you at the hotel."

Susanna could hear the suspicion in his words. She heaved a sigh, wishing these issues weren't separating them; wishing other feelings could come forth instead. "It doesn't matter whether you succeed in closing the cave down anyway. There may not be people coming to the hotel as it is, what with you warning them to stay away like we all have the fever."

He spun around.

"Yes, those people you talked to sent a letter to my father, angry about the cave. Now my father and Dr. Croghan think you only want to cause harm—that you and your uncle are planning harm against the cave."

His face colored. "I don't want to harm anyone, Susanna. You know that. I felt I needed to warn those people as to what is going on inside the cave." His eyes narrowed. "So is that why we're invited to a dinner? So they can put us in jail? Or banish us from this part of Kentucky?"

"No. They want to talk. That's what you wanted in the first place, isn't it? To make people understand your point of view?"

Wielding the ax, he swung once more. The tool came down hard on another log. "Talking is a good thing, but my uncle won't take kindly to just fancy words. He's heard all the words. He wants something done."

"But civilized people talk out their differences. And I know Dr. Croghan wants the hard feelings put aside. Isn't that good?"

"I suppose it is," he said once more, returning the ax to the stump. "I should be glad. But I know they might also be planning some trick. Something that will make us all go away and never come back. No one offers people like us fancy victuals without some other idea in mind." He eyed her. "Susanna, I hope if you know what it is, you would tell me."

Her face flushed. "Jared, it's dinner and conversation."

Jared wiped the sweat from his brow and gazed at the woods beyond. "I'll ask my uncle what he thinks, but for sure I will come."

"Good. I'm glad." She hoped she sounded as eager as she felt. She wanted him there, even if they were still at odds with each other. Just to be in his presence at the table where she could listen to him rather than the diatribe of her older brother would be a pleasant diversion.

He stood still, staring at her in a way that made her heart leap. She had accomplished her task, but she could also bask in the knowledge that a bond still existed, even if she was dismayed at him for his actions of late. He was not her man on a black horse. But there were things about Jared Edwards that still interested her, more than any dream or any other man for that matter. Maybe it was what Matt said on the way to this place. That Jared was caring, sensitive, and wanted to help others. No one should fear him but rather respect him. She hoped to see more of that kind of man in the days ahead.

nine

She was a beautiful vision to him. Her hair caught in the wind. Her blue eyes held a measure of expectancy as she extended the invitation to him with fair and unblemished hands. He wished he hadn't been so suspicious during her visit, wishing, instead, he could have revealed his true heart. He had wanted to tell her that he would run all the way if he could, dashing by horseback over hills and dales, just to dine with her and stare into her eyes. How he wanted to shout what lay hidden within his heart, if not for other things that barred the way. He wanted to cast away all obstacles—the suspicions, the rifts, the cave, his aunt's death—everything, so he might experience love and marriage. Perhaps God had opened the door by allowing this dinner to take place. He would speak what lay on his heart and forget about it. He would drink in Susanna for as long as he dared, and afterward, take her on an evening stroll.

As he rode over to his uncle's place, he hoped he could convince Uncle Dwight to accept the invitation without raising further difficulty or suspicion. He had not heard from the man in quite some time. He would have checked on him sooner if not for the recent memories of the rifle and the harsh words. Easing his hold on the reins, he slowed to a stop. The cabin looked forlorn and still, as if shrouded in a veil of sadness. He slowly approached the place, keeping careful watch, and called out a greeting so as not to be hailed by another bullet. "Hello! Uncle, you here?"

The door slowly opened. Uncle Dwight emerged, a blanket wrapped around him, shivering. Jared dismounted from his horse and stared in disbelief. "Uncle?"

"I'm sick, Jared," he said, interrupted by a hacking cough.

"Let me help you." He assisted the older man inside to a chair, where Uncle Dwight fell down with grunt. The place was cold. Jared set to work stoking the fire. Then he looked around for something to make up a cup of tea. Finding a few dried herbs on hand, he put water in a pot to hang over the fire.

"Never felt so awful in my life," he confessed. "Wish Mattie were here. How I miss her. Maybe this means I'm going to her soon."

Jared said nothing but waited for the pot to boil. He then began mixing some corn pone in an iron skillet coated with lard. "I'll get you food real soon, Uncle. Then you'll feel better." He did not realize his uncle had been staring at him until he turned to pour water onto the herb mixture, letting it steep.

"How've you been, boy?"

Jared looked up in a start. He couldn't believe the question after all the heartache they had suffered, including his uncle's abandonment. "Doing all right, Uncle," he said softly.

"Need you to help plow the rest of the field there," Dwight added, shifting about in the worn blanket. "Won't have no crop come up lessen it gits plowed some more."

"Be glad to, Uncle." Jared pulled up a chair and sat down at the table. "I've got some news, Uncle. Good news, I think."

Dwight raised his eyebrow. "Ain't been no good news around here since the day your aunt surprised me for my last birthday. Made me that fine shirt, remember? And cooked me the best fixin's I ever had. Turnip greens and her fried chicken.

We laughed and. . ." He paused. Tears filmed his eyes. "I miss her a heap. If only you could know what love is, boy. You'd understand everything I'm going through."

Jared looked down at his intertwined fingers. How could he tell his uncle that he was trying to understand—but through a woman his uncle would consider an enemy? Instead, he changed the subject. "I've been doing some talking, Uncle. With a gal. . .that is, with someone who works at the cave. And it looks like the doctor is ready to listen. They want to talk things out."

A light of hope flickered in his uncle's bloodshot eyes. His crusty lips turned upward into the form of a shaky smile. "They do?"

"That's what Susanna, I mean, Miss Barnett, told me when she brought over the invitation." He pulled out the paper. "The doctor wants us to come to dinner tomorrow night so we can talk."

Dwight coughed again. "Can't do it. Can't hardly get myself out to do my business. Maybe you can ask Higgins to go."

"The invitation only asks for us. I figured that at least I could go. This is what we've been waiting for, Uncle Dwight. I'm sure of it. A sign that could bring some changes."

"The only change I want to see is that cave sealed shut." He took a long drink of the tea. "Tastes mighty good." He closed his eyes for a moment and swallowed, then leveled his gaze at Jared. "You go to that fancy meal, Jared. Tell 'em what we want. Tell 'em they gotta do what's right for all our sakes." Dwight leaned over, his bloodshot eyes staring at him. "You tell them we don't want no more of their talk or they're asking for it. You tell 'em that."

"I'll do what I can, Uncle."

Dwight sat back. "You do more than that. You can make

Mattie proud—proud that she has a nephew she can depend on. Make us both proud of you again. It's up to you. You know that, don't you?"

Little did his uncle realize, but Jared had struggled with these very thoughts since the loss of his aunt and his separation with Uncle Dwight. He always wondered if he was doing the right thing, such as when he told those fine people from Philadelphia about the deaths in the cave or even if he was right in asking for Susanna's understanding. He'd spent many nights thinking and praying. He believed the cave was a danger and that he needed to do what he must to see it closed. He wanted to make Uncle Dwight proud of him.

If only he could reconcile that desire with his feelings for Susanna. How he wished the cave didn't have such a hold on her. Why did she have to believe that a wonder existed beneath the ground and value the cave as some mysterious yet living place that displayed God's creation?

He felt pulled in two different directions by those he thought of most.

"You'd better get that corn pone 'fore it burns."

Jared hurried to rescue the skillet from the fire. He had other things to rescue, too, like the kinship he once had with his uncle. Here was an open door back into Uncle's Dwight's favor. Yet things could easily tumble out of control like a runaway wagon careening from atop a hillside. He could only pray God remained at the reins to lead him safely through these strange circumstances.

❧

Jared stared down at his only decent set of clothes, the clothes he had worked in to plow his uncle's field that morning. He had no go-for-meeting clothes to wear to a fancy dinner at a hotel. He never thought he would need such attire, being a simple farmer in these parts. But now, heading for this meeting at the Mammoth Cave Hotel, he found himself wishing for a proper suit. A fine shirt. A coat with glistening buttons. Good leather boots. He had cleaned off the mud and taken a rag to his old boots to shine them up as best he could. A bit of grease helped to hold down the wild look of his hair. Even so, he was far from being presentable to men of wealth and power and especially to the beautiful Susanna in all her finery. There was little he could do about it. He had a task to accomplish. He was going for the sake of his aunt and uncle to see if the impossible might be made possible. And yes, to see Susanna once again.

Along the way he came upon wagons bearing visitors, all dressed in fine traveling clothes and with an eagerness to see and learn about the cave. He wanted to stop them, to warn them, to keep them away. But now he must think about this dinner. He exhaled a sigh, trying to steady his nerves. He prayed a lot and sang a hymn or two. He wished the traveling minister would come back—the one who led him to the Lord. Or his pa, wherever he was. They would know the words to say to men of power. They would have the wisdom Jared needed.

Nearing the hotel, he saw several men armed with guns, parading about as if expecting some rampage to invade these grounds from the night shadows. As he rode up, one of the men accosted him, demanding to know why he was here. Jared fished inside his pocket for the invitation, wrinkled and dirty.

"You look like a no-good varmint to me," the man growled. "What are you doing sneaking around here?"

"Miss Barnett gave me this invitation." He handed it to the man. "If you don't believe me, send for her."

The man looked as if he would rather hang Jared from the nearest tree. He mumbled something unintelligible, then asked his friend to go find Susanna. Jared waited, still and silent, until he saw her appear in the doorway of the hotel. The sight of her left him weak-kneed. Her smile warmed him all the way to his toes.

"Please come in, Jared. We've been expecting you."

He said no more to the men who continued to glare at him in suspicion. He entered the hallway of the hotel, illuminated by lard-oil lamps. In the soft glow, Susanna appeared all the more beautiful to him. She wore a dress that dropped slightly off her shoulders, the neckline decorated with flowers similar to the ones she gave to him at his aunt's burial. Again, he wished he had better clothes to wear. He would look more like a suitor to her rather than a simple farmer. For now, he forced himself not to dwell on all this but rather on the meeting at hand.

"Your uncle isn't here?" she asked in a soft voice.

"He's ill."

She immediately turned, her concern evident in the way her eyebrows drew together and her red lips parted. "I'm so sorry. I hope it isn't serious."

"I don't think so." He wanted to say more, but the words caught in his throat. Instead, he gazed at the fine interiors of the hotel—chairs and sofas of wood with the finest carvings he had ever seen and window lights every few steps that made the place seem even larger.

Presently they came upon a huge room and a long dining table. Several men in coats talked boisterously with each other but turned grim and silent when he and Susanna entered the room. "Dr. Croghan, I'd like to present Mr. Jared Edwards," Susanna said. "Sadly, his uncle is ill and unable to come."

Dr. Croghan stepped forward, impeccably dressed, and much shorter in stature than Jared would have thought. His face portrayed a certain youthfulness with large expressive eyes and a head of thinning red hair. "Pleased to make your acquaintance, Mr. Edwards. I trust your uncle is not too ill?"

"He sends his regrets."

Dr. Croghan acknowledged the other men in the room. "May I also present Archibald Miller, who manages our affairs here at the hotel, and his assistant, Hiram Barnett, Miss Barnett's father."

Jared slowly shook the hand of each man. In turn, they each examined him carefully. Susanna's father gave Jared particular scrutiny.

They all took seats around the table. Jared noted the fine tableware and silver that sparkled in the candlelight. He felt small and insignificant in such a setting. What he could possibly say or do to change these men's minds, he had no idea.

Dinner was served and everyone began to eat. The conversation centered on the activities of the cave, the rise in the number of visitors, the difficulty with supplies, and the need for better roads. Jared wondered as he ate when they would come to the matter at hand. Surely he had not been invited to hear only of their business. Or perhaps they meant for the chatter to unnerve him and make him feel even more insignificant, as if anything he had to say would serve no purpose. At times, he glanced at Susanna, wondering what she was thinking. Her gaze remained fixed on her plate, using her utensil with a delicate air, wiping her lips carefully on a linen napkin. For some reason the mere sight of her gave him confidence. When she flashed him a small smile, he felt even more emboldened.

"I'm sorry to hear of your uncle's ill health, Mr. Edwards," Mr. Barnett said at last.

Jared looked up at the sudden comment directed his way. "Yes, sir. He felt too weak to come to this meeting, but he thanks you for the invitation."

Dr. Croghan sat back in his seat. "No doubt you realize why we have invited you here to dine with us, Mr. Edwards."

"No, sir. Not really."

Croghan raised his eyebrow, casting a glance toward Susanna's father and the others present. He straightened in his chair. "We are concerned about the rumors that some wish ill toward our endeavors here at the cave. That, of course, is not in keeping with the common good or with decent men."

"I know there are people grieved by broken promises, sir. I am one of them." He caught Susanna's eye as she looked at him before averting her attention to the doctor.

"And what promise might that be, young man?"

Jared cleared his throat, even as it began to constrict. "That your cave has 'given proof of its magical qualities,' as you once said. It preserved those from long ago. It has good air. And you offered to cure the sick with something far better than any medicine."

Croghan flushed with a color to match his hair. "You remember well. I'm impressed."

"It was with those words that I convinced my uncle to part with the only person he ever truly loved, the woman who had been by his side for years, and place her in your care. But because your words were false, she's now dead. And I've lost my uncle's respect."

The men looked at each other. Mr. Miller whispered to Dr. Croghan. "Surely you are aware of the papers that were signed upon your aunt's admission to the sick cave," Croghan continued. "They stated that I would not be held responsible for the outcome of this experiment. And the sick cave was just that. An experiment."

"Yes, I know." The emotion rose within him so that he could barely contain himself. "But such things really do fall on deaf ears when promises are boldly stated before the crowds. And you, sir, don't have a miracle cave. You know that. Your cave has brought nothing but death and money to fill the pockets of the greedy."

The atmosphere in the room turned rancorous. Faces flushed. "I daresay the young man wishes only to bring threats tonight and not a willingness to talk reason," Mr. Miller uttered in a throaty growl.

"I'm not threatening anyone," Jared countered. "I'm only speaking what's in the heart of my uncle."

"And yours as well," finished the doctor. "We know that for certain."

Jared could not deny the fire that had been sparked here this night. Susanna must see the flame, as well. She remained still in her seat, twisting the linen napkin in her hands. But he couldn't worry about her opinion of him at the moment.

Croghan set down his fork and folded his hands. "Mr. Edwards, whether you choose to believe it or not, I do understand. Like you, I once had a farm to tend and a hard life to lead. Of course, other matters led to the path of doctoring and to this business enterprise. But I know how difficult it is to make a living here. And desperation leads to decisions one believes are the right decisions. But you cannot allow your guilt to overshadow the good we are trying to accomplish. Helping the sick and depraved. And offering the cave as a means by which people might seek refuge and enjoy a wondrous sight not made by man."

Jared said nothing. The food he ate turned to stone inside his stomach. Maybe he had allowed his guilt to add kindling to the burning fire. But a life was still gone. A family snuffed out of existence. And a proud doctor who still believed in his wonder of wonders, his hand outstretched to accept money, even when staring grief and disappointment in the face.

The doctor continued. "I had hoped that your uncle might come so we could share more about this. It's obvious that you both are angry over what happened. I do hope you understand my sincerity in that I wish all of this laid to rest as the dearly departed rest. I only had the welfare of the sick in mind. If my words brought forth ideas of some miracle to be found, it was not meant to be." He sighed. "Therefore, I am willing to offer your uncle a small compensation to help in this time of need, a token of sympathy for what you both have endured."

Jared looked up, startled. "You mean money?"

"From my personal coffer, young man."

He could not believe it. Money in exchange for peace, to rid them of the pestilence of his uncle, himself, and the others. "You don't mean it. You can't mean it."

Miller began to cough. Croghan flushed. "Of course I do. It is but a small token, I understand that."

"Sir, I don't think you understand at all." Jared came to his feet. "None of you do. Can your money bring back my aunt? Can it heal the grief? Can it change anything at all?" He threw down his napkin and left, striding down for the hall, the anger burning within him. It had been a trap, as he feared, an evil device, a linen bandage slapped over a festering wound. And Susanna sat there, saying nothing to the contrary.

He heard a soft voice then and whirled to find Susanna behind him. She was beautiful to the eye but, to his dismay, a mere product of this place. He realized that now more than ever.

She came forward tentatively. "I hope we can meet again, Jared."

"No," he said quickly. "This is the end. I don't see how I can come back here after this."

Her face disintegrated into a picture of distress. "I'm sorry for tonight, Jared. I wish it had gone better for you."

He looked at her, trying to believe her words. She seemed sincere, yet he couldn't help but remember her words from the past, words that spoke of her bond to this place no matter the circumstance.

"The doctor is trying to make the best out of a difficult situation," she continued. "He doesn't like to see people angry and hurt. He wants to help. That's all he's ever wanted to do. Help."

"So you agree with him? That his money is the help we need? It doesn't help, Susanna. The love of money is the root of all evil. I thought you were starting to understand that. But I guess you don't."

She bristled. "You know nothing of what I believe, Jared. You only presume to know, as you have done all along. I know I need to see with my heart instead of my eyes. I am trying to listen, to allow my heart to see. I wish you would, too, and not let your guilt blind you to everything."

When she turned and left, a part of his heart disappeared with her. What could buy him his peace? Erase this guilt? Calm his soul? If only he didn't feel so confused and so alone.

ten

Jared took the long way home that night, over the rolling hills and the sunken ground illuminated by the rising moon. What did he expect from the dinner after all? Did he really think the doctor would change his mind and close down the place he had put all his time and money into perfecting? Did he presume any of them would change their minds, even though he held out a hope that Susanna might? She would never change. Nothing would change. Her family needed the cave for their livelihood. The doctor needed it for whatever suited him. The more Jared thought about it, the more he realized that closing the cave would never happen. The cave was here to stay, as was the river bend or the dark line of trees that framed the horizon. Something else would have to change. Maybe his way of thinking. Calming his mind with the act of forgiveness. Pursuing other thoughts and dreams—of what, he didn't know. At one time, his thoughts and dreams were turning to Susanna. But after tonight, he knew his hopes of love were as foolish as the idea of shutting up Mammoth Cave. Neither was meant to be.

Jared eased his horse to a stop, allowing the animal to drink its fill from a nearby stream. If he went home and shared the confessions of the evening, he knew what his uncle's reaction would be. Unrestrained anger. And maybe a rifle pointed once more in his direction. He would have to convince Uncle Dwight to release his burden in some other way, to find comfort in knowing Mattie was in a better place and to forgive as the Lord would want. But his uncle had no relationship with the Lord. He hadn't experienced the forgiveness of Jesus in his heart nor did he have the faith to believe there was more to life than what one saw in this world. It would be like trying to convince a mule to change its ornery ways. But Jared did serve a God of impossibility—a God strong enough to cut through the pride and open his uncle's eyes. And yes, a God able to erase his guilt and renew his heart.

Jared ushered the horse back to the main road. He was glad the moon was high, or he likely would have needed to bed down in the woods somewhere until it was light enough to see. He bypassed his uncle's place and headed straight for his small cabin. He thought of Susanna living within the spaciousness of a fine hotel with its fancy furniture and chairs of intricate carvings. How could he ever think she would leave all that for his place in the backwoods? She had embraced the hotel life and the cave to escape such an existence. He had to stop thinking that God had brought Susanna to him for a special reason. He had to cease considering that she might be the one he could know and love like the woman Uncle Dwight said he needed. As Jared told her, it was over.

Jared put up the horse in the barn and went inside the dark, cold cabin. He managed to light the lantern and find a small hunk of corn pone left from several days ago. After the sumptuous dinner at the hotel, the dry bread tasted flat. He nearly choked on it, what with everything spinning about in his mind. There had to be something more God wanted to do in all this. But what?

He grabbed his Bible and began to read. Comforting words from Psalms flowed into his wandering heart like a soothing brook. He looked at the lone dried flower from his aunt's burial tucked inside the pages of Song of Solomon. He opened his Bible to that book and began to read. The words played like a love song. He could only think of Susanna's strong voice this night.

You know nothing of what I believe, Jared. You only presume to know, as you have done all along. I know I need to see with my heart instead of my eyes. I am trying to listen, to allow my heart to see. I wish you would, too, and not let your guilt blind you to everything.

Yes, he wanted her to see with her heart. But was he doing the same? Wasn't his heart filled with other things right now? Things that got in the way, like the unresolved guilt and pain he needed to overcome? *Lord, please take this all away, somehow,* he prayed. *Help me to see Your purpose and Your wisdom.*

Just then he heard the sound of horses and saw the flicker of lanterns through the darkened window. He stood and came to the doorway to see the ragged face of his uncle, along with Higgins and the man named Abe. Uncle Dwight didn't look well at all. He heaved with every breath, nearly collapsing were it not for Higgins assisting him.

"I told you this was a bad idea, Dwight," Higgins said, supporting the stricken man. "We could have seen your nephew tomorrow. It's late as it is, and you ain't well at all."

"No. I gotta know what happened with that doctor. I had to come."

Jared gulped. He didn't need or want a confrontation right now. He wanted time to think and reason, to come up with a way to present the information so as not to further burden his uncle. Now the men burst into his cabin and sat around the table. Higgins ate the last of the stale corn pone, which he seemed to enjoy. "Got any good liquor here to wash it down with?" he joked.

"I don't drink, Mr. Higgins."

He chuckled. "I figured as much. Should've brought my own. Anyway, your uncle wants to know what happened at the hotel. And I gotta admit, I'm curious, too. Imagine getting to eat fine victuals in a fancy place like that. Whoo-wee. How did you ever get such an invitation?"

"The daughter of one of the hotel managers gave it to me," Jared said, rolling a tree stump into the cabin, the only chair left to him. He took a seat near the table.

"You know her pretty good, huh? You taking a fancy to her by chance?"

Jared panicked for a moment, eyeing his uncle for a reaction. When none came, he nodded. "I like her well enough. But that's all."

"So what happened?" Dwight pressed before breaking into a hacking cough.

Jared watched him take out a handkerchief, which the man quickly concealed after wiping his mouth. "We, uh. . .we ate dinner."

"What did you get to eat?" Higgins asked, his eyes wide in anticipation.

"For crying out loud, Higgins," Dwight muttered before coughing once more. "Does that matter?"

Jared looked between the two men who scowled at one another. "I don't rightly recall what we ate, Mr. Higgins. I only remember what we talked about."

Dwight leaned forward. "So what was said? Speak up now! Did that doctor agree to close the cave?"

Jared swallowed hard, wondering how to broach the news. He prayed for wisdom. "He. . .uh, he seems to understand what happened, Uncle. He's like any other doctor, wanting to help and hoping he had found the right cure. It just didn't work out that way."

"I knew it! That no good, confounded varmint. You see, George? He's no good. That highfalutin doctor killed everyone in that place."

"He did offer money, Uncle," Jared piped up then. "He called it compensation."

For a moment the men gazed at him in bewilderment. "Money?" Abe wondered.

"He said it was a small token for all the grief we've been through."

Dwight began to cough again. "Money!" He pounded his fist on the table. "So he thinks money's gonna cover his hide. That does it. I ain't gonna listen to him no more. He wants only to buy himself out of this mess. It ain't gonna happen while I live and breathe."

"At least he did offer something," Higgins said. "Can't say he didn't. That means he cares."

"I don't care. Money means nothing. Nothing at all. And it sure don't bring back the dead." Dwight stirred in his chair, his face pinched. Jared stared, wondering if this truly was agonizing for him or if the agony stemmed from something else. "You still got that powder you were talking about, Abe?"

"Yep. Good stuff, too."

"Then I say we do it. No more talking. It's time we git going and do what we should have done in the first place."

Jared stared in disbelief. "You mean you're going to blow up the cave?"

"You're right that's what I mean. Blow it to kingdom come."

Jared looked back and forth at the men and watched Higgins, who stood to his feet and began searching a cupboard for food. "You can't mean that, Uncle."

"I mean every word. Soon as Abe can git the stuff here."

"But Uncle, there are people still in the cave. Sick people. You can't blow it up."

Again his uncle stirred. "They're as good as dead in there anyway," he muttered.

"We'll get them out somehow," Higgins went on, finding a few store-bought crackers to eat. "Even if I have to go in that place myself. Maybe git myself on one of those highfalutin tours. I'll warn 'em to get out of there."

Jared was beside himself. "You mean you agree with this plan?" He couldn't believe what he was hearing, that the man he had begun to trust would agree to such an act.

"Nothing else is gonna change that doctor's mind unless we show some force. The time has come. We've done all we could."

"But how can we answer destruction for destruction? You can't. It isn't right."

Dwight stood shakily to his feet. "It ain't up to you no more. We're doing this because of you anyway, because you had some fool notion to think that doctor could help Mattie." He reached for his hat, planting it firmly on his head. "C'mon. I ain't staying one more minute in a cabin of a coward with no backbone to do what's right."

Higgins and Abe followed him out to the awaiting horses, muttering as they went. Jared ran to the doorway, watching them saddle up, realizing the unthinkable might very well happen. No, he didn't like what the cave had done. He had his own suspicions of that doctor. But he couldn't risk harming anyone just because of his feelings. Isn't that why he wanted the cave closed to begin with? To protect and not destroy? And what of Susanna? What if his uncle's anger flamed even further, and he brought his gun to the hotel? He shuddered at the thought of the bullet that just missed him. He couldn't let this happen, not to Susanna, not while he had the means to do something about it.

As soon as they were out of sight, Jared ran to the corral to saddle his other horse. There was still time, he realized, but it grew short. He must ride fast and furious, even if it took all night.

❧

Susanna tossed and turned. Sleep refused to come, no matter how hard she tried to shift her thoughts to pleasant things—a babbling brook, the feel of the wind, strolling in the woods to look at the emerging flowers. All she saw was Jared's face, the pained expression, the pleading in his voice for her to help him. The moon shone bright that evening, casting shadowy images on the wall. She rose out of bed and began to pace. No, she did not like how things had gone this evening. What should she have expected, after all? Her father and the doctor would not heed the wishes of someone like Jared, a man below their means, a man who illustrated what they once were long ago, a man they saw as harboring some manner of evil intent. But there was a stark difference between them. For Susanna's family, their salvation had been Dr. Croghan and his offer of work at the hotel to ease their burden. Jared's salvation was peace and protection, life and not death. While she had spoken of a heart willing to seek him out, it was his heart that seemed the stronger one. He could see past the money, even the money offered by Dr. Croghan, to a better purpose. He could have money, but he wanted something greater. It both puzzled and intrigued her.

Susanna glanced out the window to the ground below. Rays of moonlight cast a veil-like radiance upon the quiet grounds of the hotel. She wondered about the remaining invalids in the doctor's sick cave and what might be happening to them there, even at this moment. Here in the hotel, it was easy to forget they existed. But with Jared an ever-present image in her thoughts, she couldn't forget what was going on. Maybe they should close down that part of the cave. Perhaps by closing down the cottages, it would help solve the problem and satisfy both Jared and his uncle.

She continued to stare out the window, pondering it all, listening to the beat of her own heart, when suddenly she saw the dark outline of a horse and rider approaching the hotel. She straightened. She recalled at once the dream she'd had, of a man on a black horse ready to whisk her away. Surely it couldn't be her dream come to life—and when she least expected it. She hurried to put on a petticoat and a dress. For all she knew it could be the men returning, wishing them harm. She should alert Luke and Papa.

Instead, Susanna lit a lamp and slowly came down the stairs, careful not to waken anyone. There were supposedly guards, hired by the doctor to patrol the grounds, but for some reason they were absent this night. Likely they were at the kitchen house refreshing themselves with victuals left over from the evening fare. She came to the side door and opened it. The single rider remained on his horse, searching every window of the hotel as if looking for something or someone. She drew in a sharp breath, wishing she knew who it was.

Then she heard it. A familiar voice calling her name. "Susanna!"

She shook at the sound of her name uttered from the night. She held the lamp up higher. "Who are you?"

The rider dismounted. He came up swiftly. "Please, I have to talk with you. It's important."

Jared! What could he want at this time of night? She glanced about, half expecting him to have brought the enemy with him.

"There isn't much time."

"I think all has been said that can be said, Jared. I don't know why you came back. You told me you never wanted to see me again."

"Susanna, please. There isn't time. I came here to warn you."

"I know. I've heard your warnings. Obviously, neither of us is willing to change."

"You don't understand." He grabbed her hand, forcing her to the path they had once taken on a night as unpredictable as this.

"Stop it!" she protested. "What are you doing?"

He whirled her around. "Susanna, they're coming to blow up the cave!"

She halted and fell onto the bench. "What?"

"My uncle wants to blow up the cave. He was very angry when he heard about the meeting tonight. He went into a rage. He had his friends there, too, including another man who lost someone in the cave. They're making plans to blow it up."

She trembled. "B–but they can't! There are people inside."

"They talked about warning those still in the cave. But I don't trust my uncle. He even said the people in there are as good as dead. If he gets his hands on Abe's powder, he might just come and do it himself. Not that I think he could right now, as he's pretty sick. But I don't know for certain. I wouldn't put anything past my uncle any longer."

She began to shiver. "This is dreadful. I don't understand what makes men do such things. . .and when poor souls can be hurt."

"Because he's hurt, too. Hurting inside, that is. He isn't a Christian like you and me. He has no one to turn to, no one who can give him comfort. He's trying to find comfort in his anger. And now it's turning into a need for revenge."

"I never thought it would come to this. I know I saw your uncle with his gun, but I didn't think the man would really turn violent." She stared at him, his dark silhouette against the dove white of the moon. "So you don't want to close this place down, too?"

"Susanna, right now, what I want isn't important. It's doing the right thing that is. And I won't have people hurt. I'd rather the cave stay open forever than see anything like this happen—or you or anyone else get hurt."

Jared's voice was gentle, sincere, unwavering and determined, willing to follow the Lord in all he did despite how he felt. He was the rider of her dream, the one sweeping her off her feet and not by some charm but by so much more. She reached out and cupped his face, feeling the prickle of beard stubble in her hand. Tears of gratitude welled up in her eyes. "Thank you, Jared. Thank you so much for coming here and telling me this. It means so much. . .I can't even begin to say." She drew forward. All at once, his arms swept her into an embrace. Suddenly their lips met. His kiss proved the grandest, the most wondrous sensation she had ever experienced.

He lurched backward as if stunned by what happened. "Susanna, I. . ." He stood quickly. "I–I'd better go before I'm seen."

She watched him hasten for his horse before she went to her father. She had to make sure he'd made his escape before this place swarmed with men and guns that were sure to follow on the heels of his warning. He mounted the animal and dug in his heels, galloping away into the darkness. For a moment, she basked in his presence, the tingle of his lips, the love welling in her heart, even on an anxious night like this. Then she hurried back into the hotel.

❧

"Lord, what am I going to do?" He had stopped in the woods, too exhausted to go any farther. He had taken down his bedroll and wrapped himself in it, hoping to catch a bit of sleep. But all he could do was sit up against a thick tree and think about the kiss. Surely it was a kiss wrought out of gratitude and gratefulness, but he knew it was much more. If it were not for the seriousness of the circumstances at this moment, he would return in the morning and take her away from that place. Maybe he still would. They could join the wagons heading to the West, away from the cave, the greed, the places filled with memories. If only it could happen. If only she would agree. He wrapped the blanket tighter around him and stared into the night that would soon give way to a new dawn. Maybe when all this was over and peace was found at last, he might likewise embrace a new dawn in his life, a light he would welcome beyond measure.

eleven

Jared awoke to the sound of a fist pounding on his cabin door. He had slept away the morning after the all-night ride to and from the hotel to warn Susanna of the impending danger. He'd tried to settle in his bedroll in the woods but couldn't sleep. After the horse had sufficient rest, he decided to pack up and head back to his cabin. He arrived just as dawn began to break.

Now with the banging on the door and the morning sun piercing through the window light, he felt a throbbing pain in his temples. Slowly he came to his feet. Dizzy, his head in a fog, he stumbled to the door.

"You no-good coward," a young man hissed. "How could you do that and to your own uncle, too? How could you?"

Jared stared at the man about his own age. A fist swung in his direction. He ducked and hastily retreated.

"The law came and took my pa and your uncle away!" he cried. "They said someone named Edwards went last night to the hotel and warned them about the plan to blow up the cave."

Jared tried to register all of this in his fog-riddled mind. The ride to the hotel and the encounter with Susanna seemed in another place and time. Then the recollection came crashing back to him as the angry face stared into his and the balled fist readied to sink another blow. "I—I had to warn them. Who are you?"

"Riley Higgins. My pa is George Higgins, and he wouldn't

hurt no one. You know, he liked you a heap. He talked about you. Said you had a good head on your shoulders and that I ought to listen. Well, I'm about ready to knock your head clean off for what you did!" The man stepped inside, throwing a chair out of his path.

Jared fell back to the opposite wall of the cabin. "I had to warn them. Your pa was in on the whole thing. He stood right here and agreed to it. I heard him myself. I had no choice."

"You're a coward," Riley hissed. "And now my pa and your uncle are on their way to Louisville because of that doctor. They'll go to jail for conspiracy. That's what I hear." Riley hurled himself into a chair. "I can't believe this. I can't believe my pa's goin' to jail. What are we gonna do?"

For a moment, Jared had no words. He hadn't really given any thought to the consequences of his actions last night. His only thought was to protect the innocents like Susanna and the people still living in the cave. He didn't want to see any more suffering and death. He rubbed the aching in his head before going to a pail for some cool water.

"You have to go see that doctor and tell him this was all a mistake. You have to tell him there weren't no conspiracy, that my pa wouldn't hurt nobody."

Jared drank deeply from the dipper before letting it fall to the bottom of the pail with a faint splash. "I can't, Riley. It would be a lie. They were planning to do it. They wouldn't try to find a peaceful way out. They were going to take matters into their own hands and not let God help."

"What's God got to do with it?" He spat out the words.

"Everything. Because He cares."

"He didn't keep my pa from goin' to jail."

"He didn't keep a lot of things from happening. Your pa losing his cousin in the cave. My aunt dying. But He has His reasons. It's not for us to try and figure it out. We're to let Him work, even when we don't know the answers. Sometimes He just wants us to have faith that He's going to work it out, even when we don't understand how He's working."

"My pa said you were religious."

"I'm a Christian. Anyone can be religious, but a Christian is one who believes in Jesus. You ought to believe in Him, too. He'd help you through times like these."

Riley stirred in his seat. "I don't have time to sit here and jaw about religion right now. I gotta git my pa out of jail. I'll go see that doctor myself if I have to. And what are you gonna do? Your uncle's dying, you know. He has the consumption. If you had any sense in you, you'd git him released. Lessen you don't care if he dies in jail. If so, then maybe you belong in jail, too." Riley bolted to his feet and left.

Stunned by the revelation, Jared stood still and silent, his heart beating rapidly. *Uncle Dwight has the consumption? No!* He recalled the look of pallor about his uncle and the handkerchief the man deftly put away when he thought no one was looking. Did that cloth have on it the telltale stain of blood, the sign of the dreaded disease? He closed his eyes in despair. In his zeal to save Susanna and others, he just might have sentenced his uncle to death in some forsaken jail cell.

Jared began loading up a saddlebag. He had no choice. He had to go back to the hotel, back to the doctor, and beg for mercy, for a way out, for another miracle.

❧

The road had become all too familiar to Jared, the one leading him to the hotel and Mammoth Cave, though he had no idea what he would do when he arrived. With his sick uncle imprisoned because of him, he, too, felt sick inside. He felt no confidence in the meeting to come. He knew what would happen when he saw that doctor and the others. He had stared those men in the eye. Met them face-to-face. They were deadly serious about their business and their cave. They would show no mercy. And another of his relatives would die because of something he had done.

The journey seemed long this time. The burdens of his soul were heavy. Maybe he had purposely slowed the trip so as to avoid what he knew awaited him. He veered off the path to the hotel and headed for the river. He would take time to think and pray. Get his thoughts together. Think of what he wanted to say. And allow the Lord to speak words of encouragement to his beleaguered soul.

The river was low. Not much rain had fallen in recent weeks. Saplings bent over the river as if attempting to draw out the life-giving water. There were few fish to be found. He paused then with the horse's hooves at the water's edge and looked at the meandering river. "God, what am I going to do?" he asked aloud. *I need an answer, but answers aren't coming. I know I have to find that doctor. I know he has no right to release my uncle or the other men after what they were planning to do. But what if Riley's words are true? What if my uncle does have the consumption? If he isn't set free, he will die in jail. How can I live with that?* His head fell to his chest, staring at the reins wrapped around his hand. He couldn't turn back, and he couldn't go forward. He was trapped with his heart caught in a snag.

Just then, a song drifted into his ears. He thought it might be a bird, so sweet and lilting the melody, until he heard words of what sounded like a hymn. He edged from his saddle and guided the horse to a tree where he secured the reins around a trunk. Someone approached, her song carrying on the wind. He waited and looked.

Then he saw her, her dress gathered in one hand, touching the water with her other hand. A hat hid her face from view, but he would know her regardless. Maybe she was his answer. He moved slowly so as not to startle her. She continued her singing, a song of praise it seemed, until he came but a stone's throw away. She then jerked herself upright and whirled around. "Susanna, it's me."

"Oh, Jared!" She hurried toward him, her arms outstretched. She seemed genuinely pleased to see him. He wanted to hold her, too, but the pain of this day kept his arms at his side, even as she embraced him. Her lips touched his cheek.

"I don't know what we would have done without you. You saved us." She released her grip on him and stepped back. She looked beautiful but with a beauty marred by their circumstances. How he wished none of this had happened, that he and Susanna could go off into the Kentucky hills, get married, and make a home for themselves. They would live far away from caves and death and jail cells and consumption and everything else wrong in this world.

"What's the matter?"

She asked it with such innocence, he could scarcely believe it. Surely she must have heard what happened. He avoided her gaze and looked out over the river once more.

"Jared? What is it?"

"My uncle. Higgins and the others. That doctor had them arrested."

She stood still and silent.

"Higgins's son told me they're gonna be taken all the way to Louisville. That's where the doctor's from. He knows the law there. He's going to have them put in jail."

She continued to remain quiet, in another silent vigil. If only she would say something, anything that would ease the burden in his heart and set them all free.

"All they needed was a warning," Jared went on. "They didn't need to be arrested. They didn't do anything. And now I found out my uncle has the consumption. I need to find that doctor and tell him. I need to make him understand that my uncle won't survive jail." He kicked at the ground. "But no one here cares about that. You said you've tried to understand. . ."

"Yes, I have."

"It's hard unless you've lost someone you love and then watch others fall because of it. I don't know why this is happening. I thought I did everything God wanted me to do. I talked my uncle into letting my aunt go to that cave after hearing the doctor speak. I thought it was the right thing to do. Then Aunt Mattie dies. And now I'm in the same place with my uncle. I thought I was doing the right thing by coming to warn you. And now my uncle is going to die because of it."

"You can't blame yourself for any of that, Jared. You've done what is right."

"Then why is this happening, Susanna? Why isn't any good coming from this? Why are people dying?"

"I don't know. God knows what our lives will look like once He's done working on them, as my mother used to tell me. He knows the past, the present, the future. I don't think it was a mistake that your aunt came here. I don't believe in chance. If we really are God's, He has a plan for each of us. And His reasons."

Jared tried to listen, but the emotion of the moment proved too far-reaching. "I have to find Dr. Croghan and tell him to release my uncle. Do you know where he is?"

"Most likely he is in the cave. I haven't seen him this morning."

"If I don't find him, another life is going to be snuffed out. Another life that could have been saved." Jared began heading back to his mount, even as he heard Susanna's footsteps following him in the grass.

"Jared, everyone here is very anxious. There are many men on guard everywhere. The hotel, the cave. If you try to enter the cave to see the doctor, they will arrest you, too."

"Then help get me into the cave, Susanna. Help me find a way to see the doctor. If you come with me, they will let us both in."

She stepped backward. "But. . .I–I've never even been in the cave. How can you ask me to do that?"

He untied the reins. "Maybe you need to see it. Maybe you need to see for yourself what the doctor has done and what lurks in there. Maybe you'll realize then that what I've been saying all along is true."

She bristled. "So you still think that closing down the cave is the answer to everything. You say it's to keep out danger. But I think the doctor said it all correctly. You only want to shut up the guilt in your heart. You don't want to deal with it face-to-face. And if you keep trying to do this, it will only eat you away to nothing."

He dropped the reins. His face flinched with the pain of her words. Yet he refused to yield. "I will go myself if I have to and find that doctor. I'll get those sick people out of there."

"And then what, Jared? Will you blow up the cave instead of your uncle and his friends? Will you finish the job?"

They stared at each other. She whirled and began heading up the trail toward the hotel.

"Where are you going?"

"I'm going to find Stephen Bishop. He's the head guide. I'm going to ask him to help us find Dr. Croghan. Stephen knows everything about the cave. He can get us in there and back safely. Stay here so you aren't seen."

He stared in disbelief. Maybe there was a bond between them, stronger than mere understanding or a simple truce. Maybe it wasn't just a kiss of gratitude they had shared last night. Maybe she really did love him and wanted to see things resolved. The mere thought made him hopeful for the future, even if the present looked bleak.

❧

What am I doing? Perspiration beaded on her face. *Do I really care that much about Jared? Can he really be having this kind of effect on me, the kind that would make me do just about anything for him?* She hurried up the trail, past the men with guns guarding the cave entrance. They nodded at her. She sighed. Something stronger than anxiety or even fear was at work here. At the riverbank she saw a man in pain. A man desperate to free himself from his burden of guilt. A man who needed answers—the same man who had sought to protect her and who now needed her help. She was seeing more and more how much she had changed. Nothing had been the same since that dreary day when she first gazed on Jared a few weeks ago. Little did she realize what a simple bouquet of early spring lilies would bring her. Now she stood on the verge of descending into a dark and forbidden place that, up to this point, she had only heard spoken of. Could love transform a person in such a way as this? Could love make one attempt to do things only dreamed about before? But there was no choice. She and Jared were connected by God's great plan. And she would see this journey through, even if she wondered what would come of it in the end.

The hotel was a flurry of activity when she arrived. Angry patrons milled about, asking why they were not being allowed to tour the cave. She saw her father and Mr. Miller frantic among the irate guests, trying to explain the circumstances without causing a panic.

Susanna brushed by the milling tourists and walked to the humble shacks built behind the hotel. In one of them she found Stephen Bishop, playing with a little boy on his lap.

"Miss Barnett!" he exclaimed. "Ain't this a surprise? I reckon you know my little Tom here."

She smiled briefly. "Stephen, I need your help. We must find the doctor, and he's in the cave. Can you take us there?"

"Ain't no one allowed in the cave, miss. Not right now anyways."

"It's very important that we find him. A man's life depends on it."

Stephen exchanged looks with his wife before handing the young boy over to her. He grabbed some lanterns, a large metal jug, and a leather pouch. "Someone hurt?" he asked, following her outside.

"Yes, he's hurting very badly and needs the doctor's care. I know you can lead us there. You know everything about the cave."

"Yes'm, I shore do. The cave and I are good friends." Stephen paused to fill up the leather pouch with water from an outside well.

"So the cave isn't really a danger to anyone?"

"There's always danger in anything one does. It's what you do with it that matters. The good Lawd gave us minds to think things out. So long as you keep on thinking and be smart, you can make it through most everything. It's when people stop thinking that they git into trouble." He began heading toward the hotel.

"Not that way," Susanna urged, thinking of her father's

reaction if he saw Stephen carrying equipment for a tour. "There's too much commotion right now at the hotel. The guests might think you're leading a tour. Let's take the path through the woods."

He obliged. "Yep, they's all riled up today. I hear someone wants to blow up the cave or some fool thing. At least that's the rumor going around. That's why there's no tours today." He began to chuckle. "Ain't no one can blow up that cave. No siree. That cave was meant to be found and explored."

"You seem confident of that."

"More than most folks, I reckon. Maybe 'cause I've seen more than most folks. Miss Barnett, when you go into the cave, you really are steppin' into another world that ain't like our own. It really is a mammoth of a cave."

Susanna drew in a sharp breath. And now she was about to enter the cave that, to her, had only been mere words spoken by people. Maybe seeing the beauty of the underground world and the good work of the doctor would settle any doubts—so long as it didn't create new ones.

twelve

Susanna had no idea why she agreed to do this. Despite her best intentions, doubt gnawed at her with ugly teeth. Fear of the unknown nipped at her heels as she drew closer to the cave's entrance. Stephen headed down the trail, loaded with provisions that included extra lard for the lanterns, food, and water.

"I never go anywhere in the cave without my supplies," he said. "Don't never know what might happen."

Susanna didn't like the connotation behind his words. She hoped this would be an easy venture and that everything would go well between Jared and the doctor so that her own relationship with Jared might prosper. She wanted to see the rift gone and a love between her and Jared take its place. The journey between them had been tenuous at best. Now she was ready to stand on firm ground.

When they came to the cave entrance, Susanna motioned for Stephen to wait while she hurried down to the Green River. Jared was there where she'd left him, pitching stones into the water, looking thoughtful and even a bit lost. "We're ready," she said breathlessly. "I have a guide."

Jared followed her up the wooded path. "You didn't tell the guide why we wanted to see the doctor, did you?"

"I only told Stephen we needed to find Dr. Croghan, that someone was sick. Stephen knows everything about the cave. He's been exploring it for many years now."

Jared said little. No doubt his mind was preoccupied by

everything that was happening. She wished the difficulty would draw them closer instead of pushing them apart. After last evening and the kiss they'd shared, she felt certain God had brought them together for a purpose. Though Jared had not been the one she once envisioned in her dreams, even if he did own a horse as dark as midnight, there were things about him that attracted her. He was not pretentious. He held no lofty ambitions. He was straightforward in thought and deed, commanded by God who flowed like a river in his heart. Isn't that all she really needed? Simplicity. Determination. A fine Christian character. And at this moment, one who needed her as much as she needed him.

"Is that Stephen?" he inquired, acknowledging the rugged black man who stood patiently waiting for them.

Susanna nodded. Before they could say anything else, a party of four men came hurrying down the trail, armed with rifles. She heard Jared inhale a deep breath and look back to the river. His apprehension grew so thick she could almost touch it.

"What's going on here?" one of the men barked. "No one is allowed inside the cave on the orders of Mr. Miller and Mr. Barnett."

"If you please, I am Mr. Barnett's daughter. I asked Stephen to guide us to the doctor in the sick cave. We have need of his skill as soon as possible."

The man tipped his hat at her before giving Jared a look-over. "Who's he?"

She glanced over at Jared to see the concern clearly written in his eyes. "He's the one whose relative is in need of the doctor's care. The doctor knows his family quite well. Stephen agreed to take us there."

The men looked at each other and shrugged. "All right, but be careful."

Breathing a sigh of relief, Susanna offered a smile of encouragement. “Shall we be going then?”

Stephen led the way down the sloping trail to the gaping hole of the cavern's entrance. A cool gust greeted her, along with the steady trickle of water. Just then, she felt a brief touch on her arm and glanced back to see Jared's luminous eyes staring into hers.

“Thank you, Susanna. I thought for a minute this might all be a trap.”

The mere notion made anger well up in her heart. “If you think that, then you really don't know me at all. You only see me as this.” She pointed to the dark entrance. “Something black and terrible. Maybe we do need to go in there so God can open both our eyes to the truth.”

Stephen lit the lanterns. “Each of you needs to carry a lantern,” he instructed. “Gets dark in there mighty quick. You won't see nuthin' without them.”

The dripping of water and the cool dampness already sent a shiver running through Susanna and a wish that she had donned one of the cave costumes the visitors wore. Maybe her chills were due more to a fear of the unknown than the temperature of this place.

Jared was pointing at some long wooden tubes and what looked like boxes lined against the side of the cave. “What's all that for?” he asked.

“Folks lookin' for saltpeter around 1812 or thereabouts—during the war,” Stephen said. “They dun got heaps of it from the cave, I hears. Hauled in the dirt from way back in the cave and brought it here to work it out. Once the war ended, they stopped fetchin' it, and folks came just to see the cave itself. And a fine cave it is, too.”

Jared rushed on. “Is there really a bottomless pit in here

somewhere, Stephen? And fish without eyes in some underground river?"

Stephen laughed. "So you know things about this place already. Who told you all that?"

"Matt. He said you know everything about it. That you've been to places in the cave no other man has seen."

"Well, if it weren't for the sick folk you got and you needin' to find the massah right quick, we could do a little exploring. But I knows we got important things to do."

Susanna couldn't see Jared's reaction for the small amount of light generated by the lanterns, but she could sense it. Their entry into this dark place had ignited some strange curiosity within him, like a flame of fire bursting to life in a lantern. She wondered about him, even as she felt her own anxiety increase. To her, this dark, dank, cold place was alive, a breathing monster of sorts, ready to swallow them up if they were not careful. She drew closer to Jared, seeking his warmth and protection, even as he continued to pepper Stephen with questions.

"How far is it to the sick area?" he asked.

"Maybe a mile. Hard to say." He then stopped. "We call this part of the cave the Rotunda."

Jared held up his lantern, the light glinting in his wide eyes. "It must be a big room. I can hear the echo of my voice."

"I'll show you how big." Stephen fumbled with a long stick and the lantern. In one sudden motion, Susanna saw something all aflame fly high into the air before them.

"This is amazing," Jared answered under his breath.

Susanna watched the change in Jared with confusion. The cave had begun to do a work in a way she had never anticipated. Where was the man who despised this place? The one who believed it was dangerous? The one who wanted to see it closed? She dearly wanted to ask him but instead concentrated on the dirty path before her, all the while sensing her own growing displeasure with the passages that seemed to close in around her.

After a time of muted silence, Jared turned. "Susanna? Are you all right?"

She was fumbling with the lantern while trying to keep her dress from dragging in the dirt. She was glad for his concern but less so about his zealousness for this place. "I'm just surprised how eager you are to see the cave."

He didn't seem to hear her as, once again, he hurried up to Stephen's side and asked him about the guide's adventures in the deep. Only when they came to a place Stephen called the Church, where the invalids celebrated services with a minister, did Susanna find a bit of comfort in the dismal surroundings.

Jared ran ahead. The lantern illuminated his excited features as he came before the rocky pulpit. "So this is where the ministers stand to preach," he exclaimed as if trying to envision such a meeting.

"You thinking you might become a minister like that?" Stephen wondered with a chortle.

For an instant there was silence. Susanna could see the question had begun to spin interest within Jared. "A minister," he repeated. "Preaching the light of Christ in a dark place such as this. You've given me something to think about, Stephen. Maybe you were sent from the Lord."

He laughed outright. "Ha! When we see the massah there, you tell him you said that. Tell him that I, Stephen Bishop, was sent from the Lawd." He turned thoughtful. "If only it were true. Then I'd be no one's slave, no sir."

The comment cut Susanna to the quick. She saw Jared abandon the rocky pulpit to approach the guide. "I know," he told Stephen softly. "Men are men. They shouldn't be owned by others, except as slaves of righteousness. But I know, too, that the Bible talks about being a servant. We're all supposed to be servants one to another, Stephen. And I think you are doing something great here. Who else could do the work of discovering what God has created under the ground?"

"Tell that to my missus. My massah gives me free rein to explore my cave, but my wife, she sees my work as fool's work. 'Why you go down there, Stephen?' she says. 'You'll go down there and one day you ain't nevah coming back. Then what am I gonna do? I'm gonna have to raise Thomas all by my lonesome, and you be some kind of statue down in that hole, turned to stone, you will.' " He sighed. "But it's in my blood. I go where the good Lawd leads. And I keep finding things."

"Please," Jared prodded. "Tell me what else you've found?"

His eyes gleamed. "Just you wait."

They continued on. The rocks shifted and clinked together beneath Susanna's shoes. She felt like she was balancing on some rickety log across a creek, certain she would lose her footing. The lanterns began to flicker as the men suddenly turned right, off the main path.

"Oh no," she moaned in dismay. "Jared! Where are you?"

He didn't answer but had disappeared up a side passage. Slowly she inched her way along, trying to keep the lantern before her to find the way. This is how it had always been with Jared, trying to follow him amid the dinginess of life to see what awaited them both. It happened after his aunt's burial and continued on even now, chasing him over hills and dales and now through the cave. At this point, tired and quite disheveled, she wasn't certain she wanted to follow him much longer.

When she caught up with them, the men were pointing at

the cavern ceiling. Stephen had lit a torch and was showing Jared strange black markings from travelers of the past—etchings written onto the rock's smooth surface for all time. She saw names and dates, a few pictures and other symbols, some recent, others from several years back, and even by a former owner of the cave, all bearing the mark of their presence here.

"I would like to write my name up there," Jared said wistfully. "Maybe one day I'll come back and do it."

"And what will you write?" Susanna asked. "Jared Edwards, 1843? A cave of death?"

He whirled then, the excitement in his eyes suddenly vanishing.

"You told me so yourself."

The lantern shook in his hand. "Susanna. . . ," he began, the doubt evident in his voice.

"I'm only repeating what you once told me. But now I think we should be seeing about your uncle rather than finding places like this. Don't you?"

"We be at the sick cave right soon," Stephen promised.

Jared turned away. Nothing more was said as they retraced their steps back to the main tunnel. Susanna knew her words had buried the eagerness he held for the cave. But wasn't he here to accomplish a purpose? She shivered as the cold began to seep into her. She found nothing exciting about this place, only dreariness that reminded her of a stormy night. The sooner they embraced the sunshine once more, the better she would like it.

All at once, she began to smell the pungent odor of burning fires. Susanna choked and coughed as smoke filled the cavern interiors. The flicker of firelight danced across the steep walls as a stone hut came into view. Stephen stopped one of the attendants to inquire as to Dr. Croghan's whereabouts, while Susanna gazed at the humble structures where the consumption invalids lived. Only a few of them still remained. The first huts were empty. Then she saw a bone-thin figure of a man, his beard long, his clothing dirty. He stood in the doorway of a hut, his cough biting the air. It was an image she might have conjured in a nightmarish dream. Then she saw another invalid, similar in appearance. These were not people. They were ghosts in a way, ravaged by their disease. She bit her lip to keep her emotions at bay and went off to sit on a rock.

Meanwhile, Jared roamed among the huts, talking to a few of the people who still lived in their underground dwelling. Most were unwilling to converse, but he found one man eager to share. She watched from afar as they talked in earnest. Jared nodded, pointing at a wooden hut in a distance, perhaps the very hut where his aunt once lived. She tried to understand the changes in him—from a man once angry over the existence of the cave to one so fascinated that he had nearly forgotten his reason for being here. Moreover, when she examined herself, she saw one who wanted to support the cave with everything in her, only to find herself distressed by the disease and the darkness. She found little glory in a place marred by dripping water and the reality that some strange cave had consumed her life.

Stephen approached her then, taking up her lantern so he could refill it with lard oil. "No one here's seen the massah yet," he said. "He comes by in the afternoon or thereabouts. Seeing as that fellar with you is interested in the bottomless pit and all, I could take you to see it 'til the doctor comes."

"I'd rather leave this place," she declared. "I've seen enough." It had been more than enough—the darkness, the cold, blackened names on the ceiling, the sickly ones.

Stephen nodded and left. Jared soon ventured over to where she was keeping a lonely vigil on a stone bench of sorts. "Susanna, I'd like to go with Stephen. I want to see what else this cave has while we wait for the doctor to come. He's going to show me the bottomless pit and the river. It isn't far."

"What happened, Jared?" she chided. "So this isn't such a terrible place, after all? A cave that should be closed forever?"

"I was wrong to say all that without finding out more about this place," he admitted, sitting down beside her. She was thankful for his presence, even if his unusual fascination with the cave confused her. "There is much more here than I ever realized." He paused for a moment. "But I also need to tell you what happened, Susanna. One of the men in the sick cave knew my aunt. He told me things I needed to hear." He picked up a smooth stone from the cavern floor. His dark eyes danced in the firelight. "I think God is telling me it was all right to have my aunt come here. That she didn't die unhappy but happy, even if the cave didn't cure her." He blew out a sigh. "If only I could convince my uncle. Maybe if I could bring him here and have that man tell him what Mattie said before she went to be with the Lord." He regarded her. "Susanna?"

"I hear you, Jared. I'm glad you talked to the man."

Suddenly his hand gripped hers and held it. "So while we are waiting for the doctor to come, let's go see what else is in the cave. You need to and so do I."

"I don't need to see anything more."

He stared for a minute. "This place upsets you that much? Why?"

How could she tell him she'd rather not walk about in darkness, that she preferred the light, the sunshine, the warmth, spring flowers, and a babbling brook at her feet?

"Anyway, I don't want you leaving this place alone. If you want to go back, we will. We can see the doctor at the hotel."

His concern for her felt like a warm wind passing over her heart. But she knew he had a renewed eagerness for exploration. Was it right for her to be so selfish? *What should I do, Lord?* Scripture filled her thoughts. *He has not given me the spirit of fear but of power, of love, of a sound mind.* He had bestowed His power through grace, the firmness of mind, and above all, His love to keep her safe. If Jared wanted to go, she would swallow down her apprehension. "All right. I'll go a little further."

He leaped to his feet as though her words were like horehound candy to him. He smiled. "I'm glad." He picked up her lantern. "I'll stay with you every step of the way. We won't go very far. Just to the river and then we'll come back here so I can talk to the doctor and resolve everything."

His voice was persuasive, his hand firmly holding hers, his eyes warm. She was glad she decided to continue on. As it was, she could not leave this place alone, as he'd said, nor could she stay here among the sick. Instead, she prayed for the will to endure and for excitement to well up within her as it had in Jared.

thirteen

He had been mistaken. Dreadfully mistaken. He wished now that all the words, the actions, the things he had whispered in the night and spoke aloud in the day could be undone. All the words about a dangerous cave, a cave of death, a cave no one should ever see again—he was wrong about it all. Never in his wildest imagination did he expect to find such a place beneath his feet. Yes, he had been grieved, guilt ridden, overwhelmed by his aunt dying in such a place. And yes, he wanted to see the cave closed. But having begun to experience this place for himself, there was so much more here than he ever realized. He could no longer harbor the anger or the guilt. Everything had been confirmed by the sickly man, sitting before one of the wooden huts, thin and dejected but with a willingness to talk. He was the sign Jared desperately needed.

"Shore I remember Mattie," the man told him when Jared inquired. "So she was yer aunt, eh? A fine lady. Good cook, too. But real sick. She was glad to be here, though. She knew she was a burden to everyone on the outside. Here in the cave, she was one of us. We all understood each other and what we were going through. She said she was glad her husband couldn't see her like this—glad that she was here with us who also had the sickness. And she died like she lived, real peaceful-like."

Jared felt the burdens fall from him upon hearing these words. All the past inhibitions with this place of death faded, as well as the guilt. Mattie had been glad to be here. She was at peace. Everything was all right. He felt renewed in his spirit and ready for whatever came next.

Now, if he could only understand Susanna. Her strange reaction to the cave puzzled him. Out of everyone, she should have the most exuberance for this place. It was her livelihood, after all. The place that brought her fine things and made her who she was. But as this place brought new knowledge to him, it seemed to birth within her fear and uncertainty, reactions neither of them expected.

When the time came to depart, Susanna was on her feet, lantern in hand, ready to follow Stephen and Jared down another tunnel and to another new wonder. He hoped as time passed he could ease her fears, which seemed as cold as the rocky walls. If only she could see this place as he did, like a person awakening to a new dawn, eager to marvel at God's handiwork carved from solid rock. But he also felt the need to protect Susanna. To care for her. To make certain nothing harmed her. He would leave the cave in an instant if he felt she was threatened by it. He knew that now, after seeing her vulnerability in this place. He would protect her with everything in his power and beyond.

He walked beside her, his hand holding her arm to steady her gait on the shifting rocks. She murmured how her shoes were not made for this kind of adventure. When he asked again if they should leave, she shook her head. "No, I will do this," she said. The lantern light reflected the determination in her face. If not for the excitement of the surroundings, he might have been inclined to gaze at that pretty face even longer, allowing his heart to absorb its beauty, maybe even succumb to the feel of her lips on his. But now, they were on an adventure of the body and the spirit. There would be a time and place for such things again.

"Yonder is the bottomless pit," he heard Stephen say. Susanna stopped in her tracks, holding up her lantern. Scanning the deep pit, they heard a trickling of water far below the wooden bridge where they stood. She sucked in her breath and gripped Jared's hand.

"I can't cross this," she murmured, even as Stephen easily ambled over the makeshift bridge to wait on the other side.

"Susanna, you see how Stephen crossed it safely. I'll go each step with you." *Every step in life together, if you'll have me*, he thought.

"I don't like the idea of some bottomless pit under me," her voice faltered. She gripped his arm. "Just help me across so I don't need to look down."

He smiled at her willingness to go forward, even if she felt uncertain. She trusted him. How he prayed for it, especially after he'd endured his uncle's scorn and ridicule as he'd called Jared an untrustworthy fool. With confidence, Jared took her lantern in his hand and, with slow steps, helped her across the bridge.

"This is sure a better bridge than what I first used to cross this here pit," Stephen said with a laugh when they had made it over the chasm. "Why, I only had long tree poles then and had to scoot my way to the other side."

Susanna shuddered at the thought, staring straight ahead, refusing to look back at what they had just traversed. "I can't believe young ladies actually do these tours."

"They do indeed, Miss, and they enjoy it, too. So, as I tell them, just enjoy yourself. There ain't nuthin' like it." He began to whoop and cheer as if to settle any remaining fear and uncertainty.

Jared returned Susanna's lantern to her. In its flickering light, he saw her smile at the man's antics. "He is a good guide," she agreed. "No wonder everyone loves him."

Dare I say that I think I'm also falling in love with you, Susanna? Jared thought. Maybe when all this was done, God would show them their future through His unfailing mercy, a mercy that Jared had witnessed time and time again. As scripture said, His faithfulness was new every morning. He would bring to pass His will for their lives. How Jared prayed that God's will also included Susanna.

"Winding Way is up ahead," Stephen announced. "Be careful here. The passage is real narrow, and you need to stoop there some."

Jared took his time maneuvering through the narrow crevice between the rocks. Susanna murmured in dismay as the sharp edges of rock rent her dress and her lantern banged against the stone. He ducked beneath the rock that jutted low from the ceiling, looking back several times to make sure Susanna was still with him. "How did you ever find this passage?" he asked Stephen.

"Twernt easy. I was dun buried up to my chest here." Stephen paused. "I had to dig it out."

"Then how did you know it was even a safe passage to walk through?"

The lantern illuminated the sheepish grin on his dark face. "That twernt easy neither," he only repeated. "But I dun looked at my chest and then at my feet. I saw the dirt there, but the way the rock came down and separated at my feet, I said to myself, this here's a passage. And if it's a passage, I'm gonna find a way to git through so's I can see what's on the other side."

Jared admired the man's tenacity. *If only I could be so determined to conquer life's struggles, to find a passageway even if buried chest deep in trials and tribulations.*

"Jared, I'm caught!" Susanna exclaimed.

He helped her undo the hem of her dress, which had snagged on the jagged rocks. "So is this what you wanted to show me?" she asked. "That I should release my vanity to God by letting it all be wasted in this place?" She showed him her dress, torn and dirty from their ramble in the cave.

He had no words to offer. He only followed Stephen deeper into the darkness. Except for their breathing and the sound of movement, the cave had a distinct stillness he couldn't quite fathom. There were no bird songs here, no tree limbs swaying in the breezes, no sound of rushing wind, no braying of animals. Only a silence such as he had never before experienced. Oh, he'd experienced the silence of his cabin at times. But there were always noises from an active and living world. Here, there was nothing. Nothing, that is, until the sound of trickling water broke the barricade of silence. Stephen pointed out a small cascade falling from above that fed the underground river. To Jared, it played like a soothing melody, interrupting the awful quiet they had come to witness along the journey. He was glad for Susanna's hand on his and patted hers in reassurance. He heard her sigh, even as she slipped a little on the muddy trail. He glanced down to see the front of her dress smeared with mud. She was right. There was no vanity to be had in a place like this.

"This here's the river," Stephen said, shining his lantern. "Look real close and you can see some of the critters that live here."

Jared left Susanna to stare into the water, perfectly still like green glass but for the minute ripples that gave proof of life. White crayfish scurried about in the light of the Stephen's lantern. And something else floated lazily in the waters, oblivious to their presence.

"They ain't scared' a nuthin'," Stephen said with a laugh. "You see why?"

"They have no eyes!" he said in glee. "The eyeless fish!"

"Jared?"

A soft voice broke the moment. Susanna sat huddled by a rock, trying to hold her lantern in her trembling hands. "I'm getting cold. Can we leave now?"

"Of course. Stephen, we need to go back. I'm sure the doctor is probably in the sick cave by now."

Stephen obliged. "I was thinking of catching one of these critters for my son. Iffen the lady here wouldn't mind?"

Susanna shook her head and managed a shaky smile. "Of course not." She began to tremble, even as Jared draped his arm around her, hoping to ward off the chill. "G–go and see the fish, Jared. I'm sure you want to."

"I'll see it when Stephen catches one. We'll wait here. It's pretty muddy anyway. A person could slip and fall very easily."

Just then there came a terrific splash. Jared whirled, even as Susanna cried out. They both hurried to the river's edge. Stephen was in the river, his arms flailing, the bags he wore pulling him down into the murky depths. "Can't keep my head above," he sputtered.

"Stephen, take off those satchels and give me your hand!"

Jared reached out his hand and managed to clasp the guide's hand, asking God for help. Slowly he dragged the man to the rocky shore where, to his amazement, Susanna was there to help. Together they managed to heave Stephen to safety onto a muddy rock.

"It's my ankle," Stephen murmured. "Fool thing. Foot gave out on me and I fell. I've done walked miles and miles in this place and never had this happen."

Susanna held up the lantern as Jared fumbled with the

man's shoe. "I can't tell if it's broken," he said, feeling the anklebones. "Can you walk?"

Jared and Susanna helped him to a standing position. "Don't rightly know if I can make it back to the sick room," he said, hobbling along. "Hurts something fierce."

"I'll go for help," Jared decided. "We didn't come too far. Susanna can stay here with you."

"I want to come, too," Susanna said. "It's too cold and I. . ." She hesitated.

"Take her with you," Stephen assured him. "I'll be fine and dandy. Ain't too far to that there sick cave. You can find it easy enough. Just go back to that River Hall a spell, through Winding Way, and over the bottomless pit. You remember."

Jared looked between the injured man and Susanna, then took Susanna's hand in his. "You're sure you'll be all right, Stephen?"

He began to hoot. "Lookie here. I's stayed by myself in this place longer than anyone. Like I done told the lady here, the cave and I are friends of a sort. You go on. I'll be fine."

Jared nodded, feeling a bit more relieved, if not bewildered, by this sudden turn of events. With Susanna close behind, they cautiously ventured back through the passageway.

"Can we find our way to the sick cave, Jared?" Susanna asked, the concern evident in her voice.

"Of course." Gone was the excitement and adventure of a new and different place. Now he had a mission to fulfill and responsibilities resting squarely on his shoulders—to find help for Stephen and to safeguard Susanna through this rocky maze. When they arrived in River Hall, as Stephen called the room, he breathed easier. Looking about, he saw a passage to his left and continued on with Susanna following his every step. They would be back in the sick part of the cave very soon if all went well.

After some time he paused, perplexed. He held up the lantern even higher. They had not yet come to the narrow passage of Winding Way that once hugged them close. Nor did any of this part of the cave look familiar.

"What's the matter?" Susanna asked.

"Just looking to see where we're at," he said, trying to keep his voice as calm as he could muster. But inwardly he began to panic. Nothing looked right. Every corridor seemed the same. Where was the passage Stephen had showed them, the one the man dug out with his bare hands? He wished then he had asked for better directions. But the man had confidence in him, and he'd felt confident, too. . .until now.

"Where are we?" Susanna asked, shivering once more.

"I'm sure we're close to Winding Way and the bottomless pit," Jared answered. He moved tentatively forward until he came to a junction of three passages.

"Which way do we go?" Susanna asked.

He wondered the same thing.

"Don't you remember?" she pressed.

His thoughts became a jumbled mess. Nothing looked right in the lantern light, but he couldn't tell Susanna that. She trusted him, as did Stephen. "We'll keep going." The passage he chose remained wide and long, concerning him that they still had not reached Winding Way. Finally Susanna asked to rest and found a large rock to sit on.

"Jared, do you know where we are?"

"Yes. . . ," he began. Then he said quietly, "No."

She straightened. "What do you mean?"

"Susanna, God knows where we are, but I can't find that narrow passage Stephen showed us. We must have taken a wrong turn."

"You mean we're lost?" Her voice escalated as she stood to her feet. "I thought you knew the way!"

He thought he did, too. He wanted to reassure her that they would find their way out, but uncertainty ruled this dark place. The truth be known, he had no idea how to proceed. "I'm going back," he decided. "The best thing for us to do is find Stephen. Maybe with the two of us helping, we can try to get him back to that sick cave. He can show us the way."

Susanna folded her arms tightly around her. He knew she was distressed and angry with him. He was supposed to watch out for her, to be a help, to find a way through this rocky labyrinth. But he couldn't. Her faith in him was all but shattered. Maybe everything else was, too.

He began heading back through the passage. If only he had the eyes of a coon and could see in this perpetual night.

"Are you sure this is right?" came a muffled voice behind him.

Susanna stood there, her dress limp and mud soaked, her face distraught, the chills overcoming her. He couldn't believe he had let her and Stephen down. He began to pray, asking God for an answer, hoping He would somehow redeem this situation.

"Maybe we didn't come far enough," she said. "As it was, we were talking and all. Sometimes the distance seems a lot shorter when it really isn't."

He set down the lantern and promptly plunked himself on a rock. "I don't know what do," he confessed. He picked up a small stone and tossed it out of frustration. "If we try to go back, we might end up in a worse place. Lord, please help us find a way out of here." He dropped his face into his hands. He began to heave from the anxiety, pressing down like a crushing rock on his chest. He should have never asked Susanna to come into this place. He should have left her in safety outside these rocky walls and never involved her in any of his troubles. How could he have ever thought she might be the one for him? Or that he could make their relationship happen somehow, someway. He hadn't trusted God the way he should. He had trusted in his own feelings, his own way of looking at things rather than God's perfect way.

Just then, he felt her arm curl around him, her touch like a soothing balm to his dry spirit. Glancing up, he again saw the luminous eyes of Susanna in the lantern light.

"It will be all right."

"I should've never done this to you," he confessed. "Never brought you into this. It wasn't fair. None of it. You need to live your life the way you want."

"Jared."

"It was wrong to put the burden of closing down this cave on you. Foolish, really. How could I expect that, after all? This place is what helps you survive."

"It's all right. I'm not upset. A little cold maybe." She glanced around the cave. "We'll get out of here somehow."

"When we do, there are going to be some changes. And one thing's for sure, you won't be seeing me again. I won't burden you any further. It isn't right. You have your own life to live."

She stared back, blinking. He thought he heard a sniff of distress. Could it be? Were those the beginnings of tears? Tears for him, one of the greatest fools in this world? Especially after everything he had done?

"Jared, you can't leave," her voice quivered. "I—I need you."

The words jarred him more than the horror of their current circumstances. How could that be? He had gotten them lost in this rock-filled place. He had cast his cares on her, not on the Lord. He had entertained misconceptions, judgments, everything a follower of Christ should not do. "You don't need me. . . ," he began. "Look what I've caused you. Grief. Pain. And now we're lost."

"No, I mean we all need you. My family. Mr. Miller. Yes, even the doctor. Desperately." She exhaled a loud sigh. "We would have been consumed by ourselves, so deep in our own way of making money and living far from the life my family once thought was a curse. But you made me see there is more to life than this. That there is a better treasure to be found, and not just in coins or in what I own. There is treasure in family, in loved ones, yes, even in a place like this. I mean you once hated this place. But when we came in here, you were like a boy on his adventure, looking at everything Stephen was willing to show you with new eyes. You could look beyond what the cave had done to see a place God had created."

He sat there amazed. He didn't think he had made any difference. But she seemed sincere. And yes, she had made a difference, too. She had survived life's trials to live a life of blessing. She was willing to risk the anger of her family to help him and his uncle in their time of need. She chose to understand and accept him for who he was rather than try to make him into someone he was not. Maybe God was at work after all.

"Susanna, I love you."

He sucked in his breath. He had said the words! Thankfully she couldn't see his flushed face in the dim light of their lanterns. But he knew he did love her. He'd held it in for a long time, perhaps making excuses for it, allowing other things like this cave to get in the way. But now the expression of his heart came forth so naturally, as if the words were meant to be spoken here, of all places, under the earth.

And then came the response as if whispered out of the solid rock that surrounded them.

"Jared, I love you, too."

Her words came forth simply, as well, out of a pure heart. Love, even in a dark and cold place. Even while lost and without knowing when they would be found. Love that could transcend circumstances. He reached out and held her. The kiss was simple but filled with warmth, confirming what was in his heart and hers. He cradled her, hoping to ward off the chills. "It won't be long. We'll be out of here soon."

"I only hope the lanterns don't go out." Her voice was tremulous.

He held her even tighter, trying to reassure her, and prayed like he had never prayed before.

fourteen

He loved her, and yes, she loved him. Even when trapped in a pit of darkness and with the lanterns quickly dimming. Even when the fear of the unknown rose higher with each passing moment. Even when she thought no one would find them and they might die in this place. She huddled close to him. Nothing else mattered at this moment. Not her fancy dresses. Not her mother's fashionable book. Not money. Not Luke's jibes or wondering what her future held. It had to come to this, with everything else stripped away, caught here in a void of darkness, before understanding could break through.

"I wish I had a blanket for you," Jared said in dismay. "I'm sorry for this."

"It doesn't matter. Nothing matters now. I'm just glad we're together." Tears teased her tired eyes and made them burn. She never felt so weary but thankful all the same.

"I wonder how Stephen is," Jared murmured.

"He can take care of himself. He's been in this cave so many times. I'm not sure after all this, though, if I will ever come back here." Her voice heightened with anxiety. She tried to steady it, to be a strong woman able to bear up under any circumstance. But she found her resolve difficult to keep. Maybe even impossible. "I'm scared."

"Just keep holding my hand," Jared told her. "Even if the lanterns go out, keep holding it."

"Jared, if you let go of my hand, I'll die." The tears trickled out despite her effort to keep them at bay. "What if we're never found? No one knows we came this way."

"We'll stay right here. The men guarding the cave entrance knew we were coming in. The people at the sick cave saw us go down the other passage. And there's Stephen. Though I know he can't move much, I wouldn't be surprised if he makes it out on his own. He's courageous, that man."

Susanna wished she could be courageous, too, as the Bible said. *Be bold and courageous. Do not be dismayed for He is with me wherever I go. Even in a dark and dreary cave*, she thought. *Even when I don't know what will happen.*

To pass the time, Jared shared morsels about his life. His deep voice sounded melodious in the cavern surroundings. He talked about his family—his parents and how eager they were to venture westward, his younger brother and sister who had gone with them, and his determination to stay here in Kentucky even after they had left.

"But then your aunt died and your uncle turned against you. Surely you wanted to leave then, didn't you?"

"I thought about it," he admitted. "But something kept me here. Or someone."

She smiled a bit.

"When God writes your name in the ground, you have no choice but to stay. Mine was written upon this land long ago. I knew I couldn't leave it. Even when everyone else had left and only my aunt and uncle remained. I was born here. I met the Lord here through a traveling minister. Kentucky is my home."

"My mother taught me about God," Susanna reminisced. "I remember sitting by her side one day. She was teaching me how to sew, and she used it to tell me about God. 'Like our sewing,' she said, 'God is making a wonderful garment out of our lives.' I never forgot it." She became silent then, thinking about that simple time when there was only hard work to be had. There were no fancy dresses. No food aplenty. Just a hot loft to sleep in. Irritating brothers who gave her no peace. Even so, she never felt closer to God than she had then, in those difficult times. It was almost as though, when she left those humble beginnings, she'd left God there, as well. Oh, she thought about Him now and then. She prayed. But when life didn't bring any of the difficulties she had come to know, it was as if she needed Him less, when actually she needed Him more.

"What are you thinking about?" he asked, gently pushing back strands of her hair that had fallen in her face.

"How much I really do need God in my life. I trusted Him when we lived in that old cabin. God and I were best friends, the way I used to talk to Him by the stream. And, of course, I would pray that He would help me. But when I moved to the hotel, it was as if God became lost in all the finery. I never really felt as close to God as I did back then on the farm. That is, until I met you."

"I know we always want to escape trials. Trials can hurt. But it's those trials that do bring us closer to Him."

"I'm sorry I didn't trust you," she piped up.

He looked at her, startled. "Huh?"

"I knew you were trying to do good here, but I didn't want to see my precious life interrupted. You really did open my eyes when we saw each other at Brownsville. I know God has blessed me with nice things. But I know He doesn't want me to lose sight of what is important either. I need to see Him in everything. And if I do stay at the hotel, I want to be more giving. In fact, I'm going to take half my things and see who needs them more than I." She acknowledged her dress. "Things like dresses don't seem to matter as much as they used to."

"Susanna, it's all right to have some nice things. I only said what I did because I was feeling guilty about my aunt. I thought I had caused her death. You deserve to be dressed like a queen. I only wish I could offer you fine things—and more."

She sank closer to him, feeling his warmth. "Jared, you have. We can pretend this is our castle with the walls around us. And you are my rider on his black steed."

"And what would my lady wish?"

She giggled. If only she could tell him that she wanted to be with him forever.

Just then, their lights dimmed to a single flame. She froze. Fear washed over her once more. "Oh no, a lantern went out. That means the other will go out, too. Stephen filled both of them at the same time."

"Stay here, Susanna. I'm going to see if anyone can hear us before we do lose our light."

"Jared, you can't leave me here."

He left his lantern by her side. "I will be just a few paces away," he promised. "I have to try."

No! Her gaze remained fixed on the lantern's soft glow. Was it her imagination or was the light already beginning to fade? Jared called out several times, his voice echoing in the cave's vastness. She watched the flame dim even more. "Jared, it's going out! Jared! Come back!"

Then, pitch black. Never had she witnessed such darkness. At first, she thought she could see him, so close to her. But when she reached out her hand, he wasn't there. "Jared!"

Silence answered. For an agonizing moment, Susanna felt wholly alone, buried in the bowels of the earth.

Then Jared's voice broke through the oppressive black stillness. "I'm here."

She heard his footsteps and thought how he could wander

off, maybe even into another bottomless pit. "Jared!" Suddenly she felt his foot kick against her leg and his hand brush her arm. "Oh, thank you, God!" She began to weep.

"It's all right."

"No, it isn't. Nothing is all right. We have no food or water. Now we have no light. What are we going to do?"

He said nothing for a time. His silence only made matters worse. "God, please help us," she prayed. "You know where we are. Send someone to help us!"

Jared's hand swept back her hair. She felt him kiss the top of her head and then heard soothing words fill her ears. He began singing a hymn. "Rock of Ages." How appropriate for this place. She tried to shift her thoughts to God's holy refuge. A strong tower. A firm foundation. Unmoving. Solid. But anxiety came again, like water spilling over. Her teeth began to chatter.

"I remember being lost once," Jared suddenly said. "And it changed my life."

She perked up at his words.

"I went fishing to a new fishing hole. Didn't tell my parents where I was going. Suddenly it got dark. I couldn't find my way home. Everything looked the same. I saw the stars, but that was all. I bedded down in some leaves, but I was so cold.

"Then I saw this light. I thought that maybe I was going to heaven. It was like a golden light, bright and beautiful. Then it was shining full in my face. Some stranger had come up, holding a lantern, someone I had never seen before. He asked me what I was doing there all by myself. 'I'm lost,' I said. Then he laughed. I thought it was the strangest thing to hear him laugh like that. I didn't think any of it was funny. I was cold and really hungry. 'C'mon and ride with me,' he said, giving me a hand up. I asked who he was. I didn't recognize his name. I told him where my home was. He said there were a lot of people lost like me, wandering around in the darkness. Unable to see anything before them. All of them, caught in the deep and no one to help them. I didn't know what he meant. I asked where they were."

Jared paused, and Susanna heard him chuckle. "So what did he say?" she urged.

"He said, 'They're all around you. But I have a light for you. A good light. A light to see by.' And he pointed to his saddlebag. I opened it and pulled out a huge Bible. I didn't understand, you see. I never went to church. But he told me all about God right there, told me that Jesus is the Light of the world. I never forgot it."

Susanna sat there, mesmerized by the story. The cave didn't seem so dark anymore. "So he was the traveling minister you talked about?"

"And one of the main reasons I didn't leave Kentucky. This is where I found light in the darkness. How could I leave it? Besides that, my aunt and uncle lived here, too. And my uncle still needs to see the light for himself."

Susanna sighed. The chills left her. She felt warm, as if a fire had been kindled in her midst. Somehow she knew everything would be all right. She had a godly man by her side and a God in heaven watching over her. She could want nothing better in a place like this.

❧

As time passed, they listened to each other's breathing and the distant trickle of water somewhere deep in the cave. Susanna strained to hear the clamor of footsteps, to see the flicker of lantern light. She remained in Jared's arms for warmth, trying to think of things to ward off the uncertainty. She thought about her desire to meet a fine man one day, and marveled at how God had seen fit to bring Jared into her life. She wondered if there was a future for them. She knew, after today, that life at the hotel would never satisfy. She needed the presence of God to fulfill her heart's desire. He was worth more than anything. He had given her Jared in a time and place in her life when she might have lost all hope.

She lifted her head to observe the surroundings—a pure black unlike anything she had ever seen. No light penetrated this place. None. Even when she thought she saw the flicker of light, she decided it was her mind playing tricks. That is, until Jared jumped to his feet.

"Someone's coming!" he said excitedly. "Hello! Hello!"

Susanna stared until her eyes began to hurt, looking at the dim light reflecting off the cavern walls. Then there came a reply.

"Hello!" answered a voice. "Someone there?"

"We're here!" they both said at once.

Matt arrived, bringing with him a contingent of men, each with lanterns. Her father. Luke. And several other men she didn't know.

"Susanna!" Papa cried. "You gave us such a fright."

"How did you know where to look for us?"

"Stephen made it back to the sick cave with that bad leg of his," Matt said. "When he found out you hadn't come back, he figured you might have taken a wrong turn. Easy to do in this place. So he sent someone to the hotel to fetch us, and we came lookin'."

Susanna was never more relieved. She grabbed Jared's hand and squeezed it. "God watched out for us," she murmured.

"And a good thing, too," Luke said. He whirled to the men who had accompanied them. "Arrest that man."

Susanna stared wide-eyed as the men surrounded Jared.

"What are you doing?"

"I didn't like him from the beginning," Luke murmured.

"It's for the best until we can straighten this out," Papa added.

"No!" She clung to Jared, even as her father tried gently to pull her away. "You can't do this. He's done nothing wrong!"

"He dragged you into this place and nearly got you killed," Luke hissed. "And we heard how he was coming for the doctor, no doubt to harm him, too."

"That's ridiculous! He was only coming to talk to him. Please." She looked to Jared, hoping he would defend himself. He said nothing. "Jared, tell them." He only stared back with sadness in his eyes. "He wouldn't harm anyone. He's only tried to help."

"By causing an uproar?" Papa said. "By associating with men who want to blow up the cave? By taking you away from us? By causing our very lives to be disrupted? There will be no more of this, Susanna. You are not to speak to this man ever again." He nodded, and at once the guards escorted Jared back through the passage.

Susanna wanted to follow, but her father and Luke kept her back. "You don't know what you're doing. You don't know what the truth is. The only thing you know is your money. But it's poison. It's poisoned you against the truth, to the things that matter in life. And now you want to punish an innocent man." She grabbed for a lantern, intent on following her beloved and the men who held him in their grasp.

"Susanna, you are to stay with us," Papa ordered. "I am your father. And as your father, I know what's best for you."

"Then if you do, you'll let me be with the man I love!"

"You can't love a man like that," Luke said with contempt. "He's nothing."

"No! You're nothing. You know nothing about love. You think because we have come to this place that it's made us better people. That it has solved our problems. But all our problems followed us here. All we have ever thought about is ourselves. Jared lost someone he dearly loved in this place. He has no rich surroundings or nice clothing. But he is content. He has faith in God. All he's ever wanted to do is what's right. And I would rather be with a man like that than be as rich as a king." She lowered her voice. "Papa, I have always listened to you. But I cannot listen to you now. You're wrong about Jared. I only wish I could make you understand."

Papa said no more. Susanna hastened to follow the lanterns that were quickly fading into the deep. She didn't care about the cave's darkness, her feet slipping on the rocks, or the chills. She only wanted Jared with all her heart. Tears filled her eyes, which she swiped away in determination. She would not see him taken away, perhaps even to some Louisville jail like his uncle. Not while there was still breath in her. She would do whatever she must to set him free, like he had done for her.

At last, she caught up with the group as they entered the sick cave. Dr. Croghan had arrived and was talking with several of the men who had led Jared away. Susanna managed to catch a glimpse of Jared's face—worn, tired, but at peace, even with his circumstances. Murmuring a prayer, Susanna came forward and burst through the circle of men.

"Dr. Croghan, I must speak with you."

"Miss Barnett! What are you doing here?"

"Dr. Croghan, you must help us. Please, may Jared and I speak with you in private?"

He stared, first at Jared then at her. "I am a very busy man, Miss Barnett."

"Sir, I would not ask except that this is a matter of life and death."

He paused. "Very well."

Susanna motioned to Jared. They followed the doctor to one of the abandoned wooden huts and sat down. She ignored Jared, who shook his head at her, and, instead, concentrated on the task before her. "Dr. Croghan, you and I have known each other for several years now. I was the one who found you that day long ago on the road when you were pinned under the wagon. And you have been so kind to us, helping my family in their time of need. Now I beg you to help another who, at this very moment, is dying of consumption."

Croghan glanced over at Jared. "I'm not certain that I understand."

"Jared's uncle. The one who lost his wife. And the one who has been arrested. I know there were plans being made for some manner of evil with the cave. But you must see how this was all brought about by a man sick with grief and sick in his body. Jared's uncle has the consumption."

"Is this true?" Croghan asked Jared.

"Yes, sir. I didn't know it at first. My uncle hid it pretty well. But he has all the signs. The coughing. The weakness."

"I'm sorry to hear this. But you must realize that there must be consequences for evil actions."

"Sir, no actions took place because Jared warned us," Susanna pleaded.

"Yes, and the men were arrested," Croghan added. "I have tried to be diplomatic, as you well know. But I cannot allow others to commit criminal acts just because they don't like my cave."

"But you can understand where this comes from," Susanna pressed. "Out of a desperation to find healing in a time of grief. You're a gentleman of compassion. You wouldn't have built this place if you weren't. You wouldn't have given your time, your money, everything, to try and help the unfortunate. All I ask is for a bit of mercy for Jared's uncle. That he can die in his own bed and not in a jail cell."

Croghan sighed, even as he looked about the hut where they sat. "I had great dreams for this place," he murmured wistfully. "Like you once said, young man, I thought this cave was a miracle. I thought with the air and humidity that it might offer something to those with pulmonary afflictions. Had I known it would hasten death, I would have never opened the cave to the sick." He paused then, as if in deep thought.

Susanna held her breath, praying, pleading that the doctor would have a change of heart.

"I will think about what you said," he finally told her. "I'm sorry this happened. I do blame myself for raising hope when there really was no hope. Hope is what drives a man forward."

"Sir, that is why we can only hope in our Savior Christ," Jared said humbly. "I know now what happens when I place my hope in what I see or feel. But faith is hope in what is unseen, in God Himself."

Croghan slowly came to his feet and offered Jared his hand. "I do thank you for warning us of your uncle's anger. Our conversation at dinner has given me quite a bit to think about. Certainly I do not hold you responsible for any of this. You may go."

"But what about his uncle?" Susanna asked.

Croghan shook his head. "I have no answer. Right now, I must tend to the others that are still here." He left in a flourish, even as Susanna and Jared stood alone in the hut with only the distant chatter of voices interrupting the vastness of this rocky space.

All at once, she felt the arms of Jared embrace her in gratefulness. "Thank you, Susanna. I can't believe you did this for me."

"It was nothing."

"What do you mean? It was everything. I had made the decision that if I were to go to Louisville, at least Uncle Dwight wouldn't be alone. That I could be there with him."

"We just have to pray that somehow he will be released, Jared. Despite everything that's happened, Dr. Croghan is a fair man. I believe with all my heart he cares."

"If there's one person I've seen care unlike any other, it's a beautiful woman by the name of Susanna Barnett. I'm sorry I ever doubted you."

She smiled, enjoying the warmth of his arms about her. "Let's just get out of here," she said softly.

fifteen

Jared returned to his cabin to find it a cold and lonely place. Without Susanna there beside him, and knowing his uncle remained in a Louisville jail, he found it hard to go on. He tried his best to keep up both his farm and his uncle's in the hope of Dwight's return. He had not been back to the hotel in a week as the work had mounted up. But he thought about the cave and the hotel all the time and especially about the fair one who dwelled there. Not a moment went by that he didn't think of Susanna. No doubt, her father was keeping a close eye on her. Always when they seemed to draw closer, something else would pull them apart. Their relationship had turned into a never-ending tug-of-war.

Jared had just hitched the horse to the plow when he heard a wagon rolling down the road. He shifted his hat back on his head to see the dark form of a familiar man hunched over at the reins. It was Matt Bransford.

"You gotta come to the hotel, Mistuh Jared. Come on now. I'll take you there."

He stared, puzzled. "I've got a heap of work to do here, Matt."

"Yeah, but this is important. You gotta come. Miss Barnett asked me to fetch you 'specially."

He looked at the fields to plow and the wood that still needed to be split. But the lure of seeing Susanna proved too much of a temptation. Every night when darkness fell, he thought of her and the hours they spent in the cave. While the place had been frightening, it had done a wondrous work in them. The truth be told, he wouldn't mind going back in that cave to do something he had been thinking about doing for a while. A secret surprise for Susanna. Something they would both cherish forever. If he could only make it work.

Jared unhitched the horse and led the animal to the stall. He then climbed onto the wagon seat beside Matt. During the journey to the hotel he inquired about Stephen. Matt laughed, telling him how the man was already leading tours again. "Nothing can hold that man back from the cave. No siree."

"After all we went through, I wasn't sure if I should ever go back inside," Jared commented.

"Why not? Cain't let no bad things hold you back. Shore there can be things that stop you in your tracks. The good Lawd tells you which way to go. But the cave is there for us. And while some things don't work out, it's still a good place to look around." He continued, "And sometimes it does a body good to git lost. Gotta rely on the Lawd. Then you can deal with the things goin' on inside of yourself. That's happened to me, and I'm real thankful for it."

Jared pondered these words and the great work God had already done in both Susanna and himself. He had seen more than he realized. He had watched anger and doubt turn one to stone like the cave. But now he felt freer than he ever had been before. He trusted the Lord with his past, present, and future, even if his future remained uncertain.

When he arrived, the hotel was fairly buzzing with patrons outfitted in their costumes, ready for an adventure into the deep. This time Jared watched them without the animosity he once felt. He knew what they would see, after all. He wanted to encourage them to go forth into the unknown. To see things like never before. And let God do a work in their hearts in the process.

Matt stopped the wagon in front of the hotel. When he asked where he was to go, Matt nodded toward the front doors. Jared entered the hotel, remembering his journey here not that long ago to speak with the head proprietors of this place. He recalled the raw anxiety he felt. Just then, he stumbled upon Susanna's brother, Luke Barnett, giving an assistant some instructions. When the man left, Luke turned. Their eyes met.

"It's you. Well, it seems my sister is quite taken with you."

"I'm sure you aren't happy about that, are you?" Jared wondered.

Luke shrugged. "Susanna's never been happy, even with everything she had here in the hotel. At first she seemed happy. But something changed in her after she met you."

Jared said nothing. Instead, he observed the man about his own age and considered the responsibilities that fell on his young shoulders. They'd be enough to drive anyone to the ground.

"This place is fine enough, I suppose," Luke commented. "It has most everything one needs. But there are some things I wouldn't mind doing again. I miss them."

Jared could hear it in Luke's voice. An emptiness. The need for something more in life. Maybe even the longing for a friend. "How about we go fishing sometime?"

Luke stared. "What did you say?"

"I know some pretty good spots. I'll bet since you came here you haven't really had a chance to do things like fishing."

"No. I don't do anything but this." Luke acknowledged the lanterns he held. "I used to fish a lot back at the old place. We had to find our food or grow it. Here, everything is given to you. Somehow I think I miss it. Farming the land. Going hunting for game. Feeling like I'm accomplishing something."

"If you miss farming, I've got a lot of that to do. I'm working two farms right now. I could use some help."

The idea seemed to spark life within the man. "I never thought I would say it, but plowing up the ground sounds like something I might enjoy right about now."

"We'll talk more," Jared promised when he saw a door open and the graceful Susanna appear. Her smile, with her cheeks all aglow, captivated him like nothing else.

"We're ready," she said. "Please come in, Mr. Edwards."

"Why so formal?" he murmured, following her through the familiar hallway and past the window lights he had seen once before. She said nothing but gestured him into a formal sitting room. Dr. Croghan and Susanna's father were seated inside. And to his disbelief, Uncle Dwight and George Higgins.

"Welcome, Mr. Edwards," the doctor said with a smile. "I found these two men wandering about, and they claimed to have made your acquaintance in the past."

Jared hastened to give his uncle a warm embrace. Higgins pounded him on the back. "Am I glad to see you," he told the two men. Then to the doctor, he said, "Thank you so much."

"I have it in confidence from these men that they will cause no further trouble with my cave," Dr. Croghan said. "So it didn't make much sense to keep them under lock and key. So long as they behave themselves."

Higgins offered a wave, his face a wide grin. "We'll be good and harmless as kittens," he promised.

"I'll leave you to reunite," the doctor said, followed by Susanna's father. "But I want you all to know, I've decided to close the sick area of the cave. There will be no more invalids housed there. I thought you would like to know." Dr.

Croghan nodded and left.

Jared looked to see the reaction of his uncle to the doctor's announcement. He only found a dejected figure, his chin resting in his hand. When Jared came to him, he glanced up with sadness in his eyes. "It was terrible, Jared," Uncle Dwight confessed. "What would Mattie think if she knew I was locked up in some jail? She'd never forgive me."

Jared knelt before his uncle and took the man's feeble hand in his. "Uncle, I have something important to tell you. I think it might help. I was able to talk to an invalid who knew Aunt Mattie in the cave. He told me how happy she was to be there and the great victuals she cooked for them all. She said the people there were like her, that they all shared in the same illness. And she knew it was better for her to be in that place."

"She said that?"

Jared nodded. "She was happy, Uncle. I know we thought she might get well, but I think deep in her heart, Aunt Mattie knew she wouldn't live. And she didn't want to make you sad by her passing. It was all right for her to be in the cave with others like herself."

"But I wanted her with me."

"Uncle, Aunt Mattie is always here with us. Everything she taught us. Everything she did. But she's in a better place. A place of peace, with no pain and sickness. And she's running and laughing, breathing in the good air God made in heaven, free as a bird."

Uncle Dwight began to weep. "I'm so tired, Jared."

"It will be all right now, Uncle. The Lord is with us. He loves us more than we could know."

"I–I've seen it," his uncle said feebly. "I remember what you once told me about the Lord and all. And He did take care of me."

"He sets the prisoners free, Uncle. He can set us all free if we put our trust in Him." Jared patted his uncle's hand. "You know I'm no preacher or schooled in theology, but I do know if we ask the Lord Jesus to forgive our sins, He'll do just that and come to live in our hearts. Whenever you're ready to pray such a prayer, I'd be honored to help you with the words."

His uncle looked at him through tear-filled eyes. "I'm much obliged, nephew. Let me think on it awhile longer. I'll let you know when the time's right."

Jared could see for the first time a heart of flesh replacing the stony manner of his uncle. He prayed that the words he'd uttered both long ago and at this moment would aid in accomplishing the Lord's work in his uncle's life. He gave his uncle's hand one final pat and came to his feet. He turned to see Susanna gazing at him. Her blue eyes were warm, her lips parted, nodding her head ever so slightly.

"You look tired, too," she murmured. "How about something to eat?"

"I'd rather take a walk, if that's all right." He looked to Higgins who nodded.

"I'll look after Dwight," Higgins said. "You two go on now."

Jared and Susanna found a side door, and together they walked the path they'd trod in other, more serious meetings. Once again everything had changed, but this time it was for the better. The burdens had been cast aside. He felt freedom from the guilt, the pain, and could enjoy this time with the woman he loved. They strolled along, listening to the birds, looking at the colorful flowers that brought the wooded glade to life. Soon they found themselves heading toward the cave entrance. Streaming from the rocks above, a gentle cascade of water serenaded them.

"I can't believe the doctor is closing the sick cave," Jared said.

"There will still be the tours," Susanna said. "But the cave doesn't seem so dark and foreboding now, does it?"

"Darkness and light are alike to God," Jared said. "I think we saw both in there."

"Sometimes I wish things hadn't happened the way they did," she confessed. "If you had been but a simple suitor on his black horse, it would have been so easy to find myself swept away. Instead, we had to struggle until we finally came to an understanding."

"We had to go through it this way," he said, squeezing her hand gently. "Maybe we wouldn't have found out enough about each other to know that we can make it through the hard times as well as the good." He paused then. Yes, he did want to spend the rest of this hard life with Susanna. But she was used to the pleasantries of the hotel. The fine surroundings. She had wanted to flee hardship even though her brother claimed she was never truly content. Would she be content to go back to an existence that reminded her of the past?

"Yes, life can be hard," she agreed, "no matter where one is. I thought having money, a nice dress, even a large dining table would bring me happiness. But it didn't. There was something missing. In the cave we had nothing, not even light. But in God and each other, I found out I had everything I needed and more."

Jared drew in his breath in anticipation as the door opened before him. He dare not shut that door now, not when God had done a miracle in their midst. He turned then, gripping each of her hands in his. "Susanna, I know my cabin isn't a hotel. My table is small. I could buy you a pretty dress after the harvest is in. There will always be surprises for us from on high. I'm sure of it. So, would you consider marrying me?"

"Would I consider? Jared, how I prayed you would ask me!"

He took her in his arms; their kiss confirming what was in his heart—and hers, too. That love and God's mercy can be found even in the deepest parts of the earth.

epilogue

"So is this the surprise you once told me about?"

He raised an eyebrow. She'd listened to every word he had spoken, every detail, even going so far as to accepting him in marriage. Now it was coming to pass. "There are many surprises from on high, like I said," he told her.

"Many?" Her small hand tugged at his, childlike innocence dancing in her eyes. "What other surprises? Tell me! Oh, you can't leave me like this, Jared."

"You know I will never leave you."

She nodded. "I know. How I know. Even when we were trapped in the cave, even with everything happening to us, you were there. Always."

He inhaled a sigh. "I wanted to know if this surprise is all right with you. To see if you really would like to have our wedding in the cave. It did change both of us and brought us together. Dr. Croghan has agreed to it. And Stephen said he found a perfect place, too, with some grand columns, he called them. I thought with everything that has happened the cave would be the perfect place."

She grasped his hand in hers, settling any doubts. He had doubted so many times, but there was no need. Susanna did trust him. And he trusted what God had been showing them both—how a cave, though dark and dreary, can bring forth a wondrous light in people's hearts. And he desperately wanted the light of their wedding to take place there. To make their families and everyone see that this truly was a grand place wrought by God and able to bring about blessings untold.

"It sounds wonderful," she whispered, her warm breath fanning his face.

❧

And their wedding was wonderful indeed, beyond all expectation. The glow of so many oil lanterns, the very lanterns that had been their light in a dark place, bathing the chamber in a soft golden glow. The beauty of Susanna in a new dress, which she had first discovered in the Godey's Lady's book, complete with rose trim that fell gracefully from her shoulders. The moment they exchanged vows of marital love before a minister framed by three columns of rock. The wonder of seeing both Uncle Dwight and Dr. Croghan in the same place beneath the earth, standing side by side as witnesses. All the product of God's hand.

Dr. Croghan offered his hand in congratulations. "I believe we have found a new name for this part of the cave," he said with a smile. "The Bride's Chamber will do nicely."

Everyone laughed. When the ceremony was over, Jared was quick to scoop up a lantern in one hand and Susanna's hand in the other. "Where are we going?" she wondered. "Not another tour!"

"To see my other surprise," he told her. "Remember?"

Her eyes widened to reflect the glow of the lantern. She put on the cloak he gave her and followed him through the passage until they came to the chamber Stephen once showed them on their ill-fated trip. Jared lit a torch. The light gleamed off the stone that bore the blackened marks and signatures of those who had gone before them. The young and the old, men and women, each with hopes and dreams, each with a life story all their own. And now he was determined to have their story remembered as well.

"Can you see it, Susanna? A surprise from on high." He chuckled. "Or at least high up."

She stared hard and began to laugh. "Jared, it's wonderful!"

Etched out in black on the smooth surface of the rocky ceiling was a large heart and charred words preserved for all time.

Jared and Susanna Edwards.
1843.
A cave of love.

A Letter To Our Readers

Dear Reader:
In order that we might better contribute to your reading enjoyment, we would appreciate your taking a few minutes to respond to the following questions. We welcome your comments and read each form and letter we receive. When completed, please return to the following:

Fiction Editor
Heartsong Presents
PO Box 719
Uhrichsville, Ohio 44683

1. Did you enjoy reading *Into the Deep* by Lauralee Bliss?
   - ❑ Very much! I would like to see more books by this author!
   - ❑ Moderately. I would have enjoyed it more if

   ____

   ____

   ____

2. Are you a member of **Heartsong Presents**? ❑ Yes ❑ No
   If no, where did you purchase this book? ________________

   ____

3. How would you rate, on a scale from 1 (poor) to 5 (superior), the cover design? ______________________________

4. On a scale from 1 (poor) to 10 (superior), please rate the following elements.

____ Heroine	____ Plot
____ Hero	____ Inspirational theme
____ Setting	____ Secondary characters

5. These characters were special because? ________________

____

____

6. How has this book inspired your life? ________________

____

____

7. What settings would you like to see covered in future **Heartsong Presents** books? ________________

____

____

8. What are some inspirational themes you would like to see treated in future books? ________________

____

____

9. Would you be interested in reading other **Heartsong Presents** titles? ☐ Yes ☐ No

10. Please check your age range:

☐ Under 18	☐ 18-24
☐ 25-34	☐ 35-45
☐ 46-55	☐ Over 55

Name ____

Occupation ___________________________________

Address _____________________________________

City, State, Zip ________________________________